THE CAR BOMB

By T. V. LoCicero

The *detroit im dyin* Trilogy
Book 1

 TLC *Media*

Also By T.V. LoCicero

NOVELS
The Obsession (The Truth Beauty Trilogy, Book 1)
The Disappearance (The Truth Beauty Trilogy, Book 2)
Admission of Guilt (The *detroit im dyin* Trilogy, Book 2)
Babytrick (The *detroit im dyin* Trilogy, Book 3)
When A Pretty Woman Smiles
Sicilian Quilt

NON-FICTION BOOKS
Murder in the Synagogue
Squelched: The Suppression of *Murder in the Synagogue*

COLLECTION
Coming Up Short

Praise for *The Car Bomb*

"A compelling and wonderfully written piece of urban crime fiction ... With its economical and supple prose, brilliant dialogue, sharply-drawn characters and plot that keeps the pages turning, LoCicero has produced a gripping tale of corruption and redemption in Detroit."   --Victoria Best

"...a brilliantly composed and complex thriller... fast moving and gripping."   —ChristophFischer

"TV anchor Frank DeFauw is a wonderful mixture of cynicism, vanity, self-doubt, weariness and wit. A kind of local princeling, his boozy, womanizing path illuminates everyone he encounters in this tight and vibrant thriller, as well as the dark city in which it is set."   --Patrick Frank

"Mr. LoCicero's interest in his characters' motivations, as in the other two books in this trilogy, vaults him into the upper ranks of writers working in this genre...in a few carefully composed declarative sentences, Mr. LoCicero provides backstories to his often exquisitely venal characters."   --Mark Feltskog

"Wild, Crazy and Simply Fantastic. This Mystery/Suspense novel by T. V. LoCicero had me on the edge of my seat wondering what could possibly happen next...a masterful job of describing vivid scenes in short movie-like bursts that kept me captivated throughout."--Susanne Strong

"From the first page to the last, it's a great, hard-boiled romp through the mean streets of Detroit, circa 1991...my biggest surprise was that I ended up caring about the characters, none of whom are idealized or in any way made unrealistic. The dialogue rings true. The characters are flawed. The action is genuine. I literally can't wait to start the next book in the trilogy"   --James Rugino

"...a fast-paced thriller which keeps you riveted until the very last page... I can actually picture this story as a movie as LoCicero's descriptions are so vivid. The ending is a real surprise and does a great job of resolving all the loose ends...would highly recommend this book to those who like Elmore Leonard's writing."   --Eadie Burke

"No writer would want to be compared with the late and very much lamented Elmore Leonard; it would be the kiss of death because he's incomparable. Having said that, there are many aspects of *The Car Bomb* which recall the great man's style and preoccupations…It has interesting characters, clear settings, great dialogue, page-turning pace and teases at the reader's own attitudes to morality."   --Bill Kirton

"… reminded me of Jens Lapidus' Stockholm Noir Trilogy…The author has a great ear for dialogue, and I couldn't read fast enough. Five enthusiastic stars!"   --Elisa Rambacher

"This book explodes into your mind with the car bomb in the very first chapter, and does not let you go until the end. I tried – and failed – to get back to the reading I was supposed to be doing, and my study, but this book kept demanding to be read."   --Rosemary Standeven

"He's a guy you could love and hate at the same time. He has a loving family and a hot girlfriend on the side, drinks too much, thinks too much of himself. But this book had me hooked from the beginning. If you like fast-paced crime thrillers, this book is for you. I can't wait to read the rest of the books in this series."   --Andrea Knott

"WOW! Seat gripping! You really don't expect some of this to happen…oh but it does! This author is amazing with his writing skills and his books are really showing it!"   --Peggy Salkill

"I have never met this author, have not given birth to him or any of his children. This is a solid and true fangirl review of a truly fabulous work."   --Tammy Dewhirst

"LoCicero nails his characters and the setting with uncanny accuracy, pulling you under the gritty streets and into the sparkling salons…You get inside the characters' minds, suspect their motivations, and alternate between weeping when a character is in pain and cheering when another gets what's coming. This is a book you can't put down until it's done—but it's never really over. It just leaves you wanting more."--Charles Ray

"I LOVED this book…EVERY sentence packed a punch. Tom LoCicero's bio says he's been writing across five decades, and you know what? It shows. It really does. The style is impeccable."
--Bridget Kulakauskas

T. V. LoCicero

T.V. LoCicero has been writing both fiction and non-fiction across five decades. He's the author of the true crime books *Murder in the Synagogue* (Prentice-Hall), on the assassination of Rabbi Morris Adler, and *Squelched: The Suppression of Murder in the Synagogue*. His novels include the romance *When A Pretty Woman Smiles,* the coming-of-age literary novel *Sicilian Quilt,* and the crime thrillers *The Car Bomb, Admission of Guilt* and *Babytrick* (The *Detroit im dyin* Trilogy), and *The Obsession* and *The Disappearance* (the first two books in The Truth Beauty Trilogy. Eight of his shorter works are now available as ebooks. They are available as well (along wih several other short pieces) in *Coming Up Short,* a collection of fiction and non-fiction. LoCicero has also published stories and essays in various periodicals, including Commentary, Ms. and The University Review, and in the hard-cover collections *Best Magazine Articles, The Norton Reader* and *The Third Coast.*

THE CAR BOMB

By T. V. LoCicero

The *detroit im dyin* Trilogy
Book 1

TLC *Media*

THE CAR BOMB
by T. V. LoCicero
Copyright 2013 by T. V. LoCicero

For more information on this and other works by T.V. LoCicero please visit:
www.tvlocicero.com

For Patrick

detroit im dyin
only come here on a dare
detroit im dyin
dont you even fuckin care

--Detroit Street Grafitti, early 1990s

Chapter 1

On a clear, bright, early evening in May, 1992, in a westside Detroit neighborhood lined with weathered '50s colonials, squat, swarthy Arnold Russo, his eye to the Panasonic's viewfinder, backed off a low slab porch onto his neatly kept front lawn. Out of the front door came a teenaged couple, Jeff in a white tux and pink ruffled shirt, Jill in a Portofino blue prom dress with spaghetti straps that kept falling.

Arnold said, "Okay, natural now! Walk to the right."

Holding hands, the couple moved off the porch to their right.

"No, no, to the right, for chrissake!" Arnold dipped the camera from his eye to function as an exasperated director, then remembered he was his own camera operator.

Jill whined, "We did go right, Daddy."

Arnold barked, "Jesus, high school graduates!"

"Daddy, you're swearing on the tape!"

Arlene, tall and bony thin, and Mikey, a ten-year-old version of Arnold, came out on the porch. The wife rolled her eyes. "Oh, right, Mister Hollywood."

"Yeah, someday you'll thank me." Arnold shot the couple posing now on the cracked driveway. "Jesus, do somethin'. It's movin' pictures."

Jill again with the whine: "Mom, tell him to stop."

Arnold said, "Mikey, get in there and do something with your sister."

Off the porch, Mikey ran to the couple and tried to stand on his head.

Jill stamped her foot. "Mom!"

"Arnold, this is getting ridiculous."

Behind the teen couple, two doors up the street, a young black woman emerged from a house with two small children. They headed for an old maroon Dodge on the street.

Noticing her neighbors, the woman stopped and called, "Oh, let me see, honey. Twirl that pretty dress."

Pleased, Jill did a spin. "Hi, Mrs. Peoples. Hi, kids."

Her mom on the porch and Juanita Peoples exchanged waves. Arnold kept the camcorder rolling.

Juanita said, "Beautiful, honey. We're in a rush, or I'd get my camera too."

A last wave and she hustled her little boy and girl into their car seats in the Dodge and slipped behind the wheel. Arnold was still shooting the teen couple with the Peoples' car behind them.

Juanita turned the ignition, and with a huge percussion that Arnold felt in the chest, the Dodge became a fireball.

"Oh, Jesus, God!" He flinched yet kept the camera in front of his eye as a kind of shield from the furious orange flames. Jill uttered a high-pitched scream, but it was nearly lost in the roar of the raging fire. Jeff held her tightly in his arms as they both turned away, and Arlene grabbed little Mikey and yanked him back toward the house.

Thick black smoke was billowing now from the burning wreckage and heading up. As it reached the top branches of the giant Dutch Elms lining the street, a breeze began moving it off above this rustbelt metropolis going about its business, oblivious to what Arnold had just recorded.

Within 10 minutes, the leading wisp of smoke was high above a red Viper convertible moving in the same direction.

Chapter 2

At the wheel of this "Buy American" roadster was Frank DeFauw, 48, tanned, sandy-haired, and dressed expensively in a navy suit and Caribbean blue tie. Frank knew his face showed more than a little mileage, although that young gal with the local monthly wrote last week that it still owned a "charismatic edge." A glance at it in the rear view mirror told him again that she was sweet. And full of shit.

From the Viper's dash came a well-modulated radio voice belonging to a fellow he had shared drinks with 10 years ago in New York when he was thinking of taking the job at WNBC.

"In the wake of that deadly riot in Los Angeles, four men have been arrested in the beating of truck driver Reginald Denny. And supporters of Texas billionaire Ross Perot say they've filed 200,000 signatures to place Perot on the Texas presidential ballot. And that's Newsbreak for this hour."

Frank tapped a button on the radio and Eric Clapton suddenly sang with his lilting guitar, "You Look Wonderful Tonight."

Chapter 3

At the Black Knight Inn he watched the valet boys running at the dinner hour. Three cars were queued in front of the Viper as he listened to Clapton finish and give way to a spot for McDonald's. This he ended abruptly by punching the AM radio button and giving voice to an excited young news reporter who had fawned on him recently at a banquet:

"I'm live at the scene of an apparent car-bombing that happened just minutes ago on Eliot Street on the city's westside. Police are already on the scene..."

Frank moved up to the restaurant's overhang. A kid in a polo shirt with the Black Knight logo and the name "Andy" scripted below snapped open the driver's side door.

"Hey, good evening, Mr. D. How..."

Frank raised his left hand off the wheel just high enough to shut the kid up.

"According to one neighbor, a woman and her two children were in the car when it exploded."

Frank put his hand down on the wheel. "Andy, you know where Eliot Street is? This side of town?"

"No, I sure don't, Mr. D."

Frank grabbed a phone off the dash and punched in a number. "Just one second, Andy." The kid nodded, and Frank said into the phone, "Neil, you got this car bombing on the westside?" After a pause: "Okay, good. I'll check in later." He got out of the car. "Andy, I'll want the top up."

"You got it, Mr. D."

With a lithe step Frank moved to the restaurant door. The Black Knight's foyer was jammed tonight. He stepped slowly through the crowd with an occasional "Excuse me" and "Thanks so much." In his wake he left murmurs of surprise and whispers of his name. A man asked how he was doing. Frank glanced just long enough to be sure he didn't know the guy. "Great. How about you?"

When Rosie, the petite 50-year-old hostess with a streaked hairdo, spotted him heading her way, she ignored the people talking to her and moved her huge smile directly to him. "Frank, you look beautiful, as usual." With a hug and a kiss on the cheek, she slipped a proud, possessive arm around his waist and moved him through her patrons less privileged.

"How you doin', doll? Lookin' pretty fine yourself."

"Ah, Frank, flattery will get you anything I've got."

Leaving the foyer, Rosie led him past a long, dark-paneled bar. Halfway down, two heads were in a conspiratorial bow. They came up as Frank approached. One belonged to a small, slight man he despised as the town's leading gossip, the other to a pudgy, well-known defense lawyer in a pinstriped suit with a red bow tie and suspenders. Frank hoped to slide by them unnoticed, but "Wee Willie" Barnes turned on his stool. "Hey, Frank, how they hangin'?"

Frank stopped. "I wouldn't know, Wilbur. I haven't been reading your column."

Barnes deflected the venom with two innocent palms up. "Hey, big guy, I haven't laid a glove on you lately."

Frank in a quiet voice: "You little prick, if you didn't have me to write about, that rag you work for would shit-can your ass in a heartbeat."

On the next stool, Sam Dworkin, the flamboyant criminal mouthpiece, flashed an obscene grin. "Frank, you got this little guy all wrong. He was just saying how much he loves and admires your work."

"Letting him suck your fat cock, counselor?"

Frank rejoined Rosie and her big smile. She was already holding a Scotch. "Your usual libation?"

Frank took it. "Great. Sorry about that, Rosie."

"Oh, you know Wil's problem." She leaned close as they walked together and held up a hand with the thumb and forefinger about an inch apart.

Frank's laugh was raucous. "Rosie, you're bad."

Chapter 4

When Rosie delivered Frank to the prized Booth One with a commanding view of the room, trim, athletic Judge William O'Bryan had eyes only for his seatmate, a curvy blond in a low-cut blouse.

Rosie interrupted, "I think you two boys know each other?" The judge reluctantly tore his gaze away.

Frank shook his hand. "Ah, your highness, and who's this lovely creature?" She was already dipping low to get up, further revealing a red lacy item and much of its contents.

"Frank, this is Kim. Kim, Frank DeFauw."

Kim took Frank's hand in both of hers. "Oh, I'm a big fan."

Frank brought her right hand to his lips. "How nice, darling. You have taste."

Kim giggled with a curtsey. "Why thank you, kind sir."

The judge put a hand firmly on her rump. "Frank, Kim's gotta run. She's late for her class in quantum physics."

Frank raised an eyebrow at the blond. "In grad school, are you, Kim?"

Another giggle. "Oh, you know Billy. He's a big kidder."

Frank nodded. "Oh, yes, I know Billy. Nice meeting you, Kim."

She smiled at Frank and winked at the judge. "Call me later?"

"Of course," said the judge.

Both men watched as she walked off. Then Frank sat in the booth. "Tell me something. When she's coming, does she call you 'Billy,' or do you insist on 'your honor'?"

"Frankie, this is strictly Platonic."

"Billy, where do you find these bonbons?"

The twinkle in his old pal's eye told Frank the judge loved this exchange. "Man, with your cameras in my courtroom, I have to beat them off with a stick."

"Must be the black robe. Like those coeds so nuts about the good fathers back in high school, they wanted to give 'em all blowjobs."

The judge nodded with a self-satisfied look on his sharp features. "So what's in the news?"

Frank took a swig from the Scotch. "Same old shit. Coming here, though, I caught something about a car bombing."

"Really? Who the hell uses car bombs any more?"

"Those crazy Chaldeans. Except this wasn't a Chaldean neighborhood. Westside, they said, maybe not that far from here, actually. I almost left you here to cover it."

The judge's creased brow was serious. "Anybody hurt?"

"A woman and two kids were in the car."

"Jesus!" William O'Bryan shook his head, then drained the last of his drink. He waved two fingers at the bartender.

"Yeah, probably a mistake."

"I guess."

"Yeah," said Frank, "I almost got the old urge. Sometimes I think I was happier 20 years ago, when I was doin' what that radio kid does, runnin' all over town covering breaking stuff, getting it before anybody else. A big bloody rush, and I was pretty good at it."

Frank knew what was coming now. Despite all the mockery and kidding, their long history dictated a brief but heartfelt reassurance on correct life choices.

The judge on cue: "Well, you're pretty good at what you do now, and you're a lot richer and more famous. By the way, nice wrap on the Bill Hart conviction last week."

"Oh, thanks. Yeah, Christ, old Chief Hart salting away taxpayer millions while his narco guys have to go into their own pockets for 50 bucks to pay their snitches."

"God, the corruption is rampant in this town. And Coleman still calls him a good man and a good cop."

"Yes, our mayor is nothing if not loyal to his pals."

As usual, the silence that followed lasted no more than a second or two before the judge opened a new subject. "So, the book, how's that coming?"

"It's coming. I think I've talked to half the Belgians in this town. I'm up early most mornings writing, unless I was prowling the night before. So how about you? What's new? I mean beside Kim. Any scuttlebutt?"

"Well, let's see. Oh, I hear our crusading county prosecutor is about to resign."

This interested Frank. "Gant? Why would he do that? He's only been in there a year."

"I don't know. Maybe problems at home."

A waiter brought two more drinks and was followed by a pretty young woman with fine black hair and green eyes. She was holding a pen and a slip of paper. With a nervous smile: "Frank, I hope I'm not bothering you. I just had to ask for your autograph."

In a quick, gallant move, Frank was up from the booth and took the young woman's soft, warm hand. "No bother at all, darling. And your name is?"

"Patty O'Conner? I'm just one of your biggest fans."

"Well, Patty, sit here for a minute next to Judge William O'Bryan. Better known to his friends as Honorable Billy." Frank ushered her into the booth between the judge and himself.

Smiling at the judge, Patty sat and said, "Well, I told Larry this would only take a sec. He thinks it's for my mother. But it's really for myself."

Sitting again, Frank nodded at a young man glowering at them from a nearby table. "And Larry is your boyfriend sitting over there looking green?"

Patty stared at Frank for a second, her mouth open slightly. "You are so perceptive. He's so jealous it drives me crazy sometimes."

Frank said, "Jealousy can be a terrible thing, Patty."

"Oh, damn! He's coming over here." She closed her eyes for a moment. As if none of this would happen if she didn't watch. "Now there's going to be trouble."

Larry was stocky, maybe a one-time high school linebacker now sprawling into his mid-twenties. As he approached, Frank gave him a big smile and offered his hand.

"Hey, Larry, how you doin'? Patty here's been telling us all about you."

Larry ignored Frank's hand. "I'll bet. Com'on, Patty, we're getting out of here."

Frank shook a weary head at the judge, disappointed with the young guy. "Now, Larry, have some manners. Patty just wants an autograph, and I'll be happy to oblige."

Larry said, "Look, slimeball, you may impress some people, but not me. So just stuff it. Patty, I said com'on."

Frank got up to let Patty out of the booth. "Hey, Larry, nobody wants any trouble here. Patty's free to leave any time she wants."

Hoping promptness would save the moment, Patty slid quickly over the smooth brown leather of the booth. Larry extended an arm to move Frank back, and Frank shoved it away. Larry threw a wild right. Frank ducked and chopped a short powerful blow to the solar plexus. Larry sat on the floor.

Patty screamed, and conversation in the room stopped for a few seconds, then resumed much louder. Two young men in bussing uniforms appeared quickly, pulled Larry to his feet, his face beet red. As they ushered him out, Patty began to follow, then quickly moved back to the table and placed the slip of paper and the pen in front of Frank.

"I'm so sorry, Frank."

"No problem." He scribbled: "To Patty, with affection. Frank DeFauw."

"Thanks so much, Frank." Patty hesitated, wanting this moment to last.

"Don't mention it. Now you better go take care of your guy." Frank nodded at the glowering young man standing with Rosie in the foyer.

Patty smiled sadly and walked away. Frank turned to the patrons at a nearby table. "Sorry, folks, just one of my overzealous fans."

He got nervous laughter and scattered applause.

Chapter 5

In a small edit room in the news department at WTEM-TV, Dennis Clark, a 26-year-old producer in a shirt and tie, sat with an editor named Eddie. With 10 years and about 75 pounds on Dennis and much less hair, Eddie wore a green plaid shirt and thick glasses. They were both glued to a monitor as Eddie played and replayed some grainy home video of a car exploding.

Dennis said, "Oh, Christ, this is hard to watch."

Eddie's opinion was, "Awesome, man." After running the tape back at triple speed, he played it forward in slow motion. "See, they musta put it next to the gas tank. The back end goes first."

Distracted, Dennis said, "Yeah, I wonder how much of this we should use."

Eddie had no doubts. "All of it, man. This is the hottest shit I've seen in a long time."

"Yeah, but Christ, watching a mother and her two kids get blown up and burned alive."

Eddie dealt easily with sensitive issues. "So you do a warning — whatta you call those things? A disclaimer. You know, 'This may be too much for the kids, so maybe you should send them out of the room.' That always gets more people to watch."

Dennis sounded dubious. "Yeah, right."

At the edit room door Frank appeared, his hair disheveled, face haggard, tie askew, French cuffed sleeves rolled up on powerful forearms and the odor of alcohol and cigarette smoke already filling the closet-sized room.

Knowing Frank's scent at this hour, Eddie did not look up. "Hey, Frank, look at this."

"Eddie, I hear you got something hot."

"The hottest, man. Watch this."

On the monitor the car exploded one more time. Frank was stunned. "Good god!"

Finally, Dennis had an idea on how to do this. "Run it back, Ed, to where the little kid is trying to stand on his head. I think we'll take it from there."

Frank: "Where'd we get this?"

Dennis: "The guy called us. He's shooting his daughter and her prom date, and it all happens right in front of him."

"We got it exclusive?"

"Yep, even the cops didn't have it until we made this dub and gave them the original. The guy wants to be on with you, Frank, live from his living room."

Eddie: "Everybody wants to bask in the glory of the Sun King."

Frank, leaving: "Cut it out, Eddie, you'll give me a big head. Give me your notes, Denny, and I'll write the lead."

"Right, Frank."

"The Sun King reeks tonight," said Eddie.

"He reeks almost every night," said Dennis.

"Yeah, but sometimes I think the guy's better when he's tanked."

"Well, you never know what he's gonna do. And that's probably why half the audience tunes in."

Chapter 6

The large room was filled with desks and partitions for reporters, and in a C-shaped area known as the pit, several writers, producers and directors sat staring at terminals. Unnoticed, Frank walked by and announced on the move, "Gant, the Wayne County prosecutor. Someone call and ask why he's resigning."

The pink, earnest face of a red-haired, pony-tailed young woman lifted quickly from her screen. "I'm on it, Frank."

He stopped and looked her over. "And you are who?"

"Francine Rickey." With a head bob. "New writer/p.a. Just started tonight." She tried to smile but did not pull it off.

He was moving again. "Well, Francine, welcome aboard. Somebody around here must have Gant's home number. When you reach him, just say, 'Frank DeFauw wants to know why you're resigning.'"

"You've got it." This time, with Frank no longer staring at her, she managed the smile.

With his usual self-mocking, dramatic flare, he paused before heading into the hallway that would take him to the men's room. "Honey, I know I've got it. Now we'll find out what you've got."

A moment later, pushing through the swinging door, he checked out the room's two empty stalls, then moved to a make-up mirror lined with lights. He looked at himself intently and spoke softly with quiet disgust: "What a piece of work, Frank. You look like shit warmed over."

From a pants pocket he pulled a small vial and popped its last red pill. Tucking a paper towel into his light blue shirt collar, he proceeded to apply make-up from items in his leather kit. First some liquid eraser on the deep lines under his eyes and then some pancake over his face and neck. A few strokes with a brush put his hair back in place. Finally, he removed the paper towel, firmed up his tie and told himself, "Frank, you still look like shit."

12

Chapter 7

In another bathroom across the old city and a mile into a northern suburb called Southfield, cool blue eyes opened in the attractive face of 30-year-old Sherie Sloan. She was lounging in a bathtub and watching a portable TV on a counter close by. On screen Arnold Russo sat on a couch in his living room. In a corner of the screen was a "Live 5" logo.

Arnold was saying, "Well, Frank, the thing of it is, he's the quiet type, you know, keeps to himself. Friendly enough, I mean, but like the other day I seen him out there cuttin' his lawn, and I wave and he waves, and I say, 'Hey, Anthony, how you doin'?' And he says, 'Fine.' And that's it, you know. Quiet."

On the small screen Sherie watched Frank sitting on the Channel 5 news set. "Well, Mr. Russo, to your knowledge..."

Mary Scott, a handsome, slow-burning black woman sat next to Frank in the WTEM news studio, drummed her fingers lightly on the faux marble anchor desk and stared up at the lights. A stagehand got ready to help reposition one of the cameras for the break, and the floor manager spun a hand at Frank to wrap.

Talking to a monitor with the live shot of Arnold Russo, Frank sailed on: "...was there any hint of trouble between Juanita Peoples and her husband?"

Arnold, enjoying his moment: "No, Frank, didn't see that. 'Course you never know..."

Frank cut him off. "Thanks, Mr. Russo, you've been a big help."

"No problem, Frank. Any time. Like I said, I just kept rollin', and..."

Frank turned back to the center camera. "Thanks again, Mr. Russo. As you heard earlier, police do not think that Anthony Peoples was home at the time of the explosion. And they have not been able to establish his current whereabouts. Of course our

13

Channel 5 news team will continue to be on top of this story for any breaking developments. Mary?"

Without a glance at the object of her loathing, the woman smiled at the camera lens. "There *is* other news tonight, and when we come back, we'll have the latest poll results on the presidential race. Guess who's giving both President Bush and Governor Clinton a run for their money? Stay with us."

As she shuffled her script, Frank leaned back, folded his arms over his chest with a quick grimace. The floor manager finally dropped her raised hand and said, "We're gone."

From the side of her mouth Mary Scott said, "Christ, Frank, eight minutes with that asshole and his camcorder. Why didn't you ask about his hemorrhoids? Twelve minutes in and I've barely said hello."

Frank sent her a bland stare. "It's a big story, Mare. Maybe someday when you grow up, you'll have a chance at a big story like that."

Mary, with a full turn to him: "Fuck you, Frank."

Now the portable TV sat on a dresser in Sherie Sloan's bedroom; on screen was the burley sportscaster Steve Madden. Walking in naked, she moved to profile herself in the full-length mirror on the back of the closet door. The breasts still looked reasonably good, high and firm, but was the middle getting a little thick? Cocking her head, she could almost hear her best friend Anita saying, "You're absolutely throwing yourself away with this man."

Looking back at her well-turned bottom, the part she had always liked the best, she told herself what she usually told Anita, that it was probably true, but it was her own choice. At the dresser she slipped on a short, nearly transparent negligee. She was not interested in what Madden was saying: "After two rounds at the Byron Nelson Classic in Irving, Texas, Billy Ray Brown leads with a ten-under-par 132. Frank?"

Now she turned to the screen as Frank said, "Stevie, who in the world is Billy Ray Brown, and what are the odds this guy will even be on the leader board come Sunday afternoon?"

On set Madden sat directly on the upholstered seat of his chair. Frank sat on one pillow, Mary Scott on two. On the studio monitor

Frank appeared slightly taller than the other two.

Madden: "No doubt about it, Frank, he's an unknown, and they usually wither under the pressure. But it looks like they're in for some bad weather down in Texas, and there's no tellin' what can happen."

Frank: "Well, speaking of the weather, Larry is in here next with the word on whether one of those storms they've been having out west…" He paused. "…is coming our way. We'll be right back."

In the control room next to the studio, seated in front of a large bank of monitors, the director was saying, "And go." A phone buzzed in front of Dennis Clark, who picked it up and stared at a monitor that showed Frank with a phone to his ear.

"Yes, Frank." (pause) "Ah, Francine wrote the tease." (pause) "Right away."

In the studio Frank sorted his script, pulled out a page and scrawled two circles on it. Dennis' voice filled the room: "She's on her way, Frank. Also, we just got a call from a woman who says she can tell your back is bad again, and she's gonna start a novena for you. I told her you've just got gas."

Everyone in the studio laughed except Frank, who glanced up only when a worried Francine entered.

"Frank, you wanted to see me?"

"Francine, you wrote this weather tease?" He held up the script page with his circles.

"Which tease? Oh, yes, I did."

"This tease, with the basic grammatical error. 'One of those storms *is* coming,' Francine, not '*are* coming.' Singular subject, singular verb. Pretty fucking basic, Francine."

The girl was mortified. "I'm so sorry, Frank. I changed 'those storms' to 'one of those storms' and forgot to change the verb. I'm really sorry."

The floor manager raised her hand. "Ten seconds."

That was more than enough time for Frank. "You're sorry, but it's my ass hanging out there in front of a million people. If I don't correct it in mid-sentence, I look like an ignorant jerk."

Just as Frank finished, the floor manager pointed at him, and Frank's vexed face instantly glowed with a warm smile.

"A pleasant week-end on tap, Lawrenzo?"

In Sherie's living room, light came only from a large screen TV and two long-stemmed candles on a glass-top cocktail table. As she entered in her wispy gown and carrying a bottle of wine, Larry Adair spoke in front of a weather map. She sat on a couch and filled one of the two wine glasses on the table as Larry was saying, "Maybe a little rain toward the end of the day on Sunday, but most of us should be able to play outside."

Frank said, "Two more like today, Larry, and we give you a gold star."

Chapter 8

The bar turned out to be little more than a dive in one of those close-to-the-bone, next-to-hopeless Detroit neighborhoods on the near westside. A red neon sign blinked "Bar" in a small window. Above, with almost half its lights burned out, a larger sign tried to say "Marvin's."

Inside, the long, gritty room featured a scarred old bar on one side and tables and booths on the other. A jukebox filled the smoky haze with the Stones' "Rock and a Hard Place." Playing pool in the back were two unhappy-looking guys, one white, one black. At the bar near the pool table sat a scrawny, sour-faced fellow in a dirty sweatshirt cut off at the shoulders to reveal the full length of his skinny white arms. He and the large black bartender were the first to see Frank walk in.

Still dapper in his navy suit, he gave the place a quick glance-around, then sat at the near end of the bar. With a languid look, the bartender took his time to saunter up and say, "Hey, how you doin'?"

"I'm doin' good," said Frank. "And you?"

"Same here. It's Frank, ain't it?"

"Yes, sir. And yours?"

"Mine's Jackson."

"Well, Jackson, how about a Bud Lite?"

"Comin' up." While Jackson wiped and popped the bottle, the scrawny guy in the sweatshirt never took his eyes off Frank. Now he was moving with his drink from his end of the bar to a stool not far from where Jackson placed the beer on a paper napkin in front of Frank.

"On the house, Frank. You wanna glass?"

"No, thanks. Hey, I appreciate that."

"Man, we always got you tuned in." He nodded toward a TV set hung above the bar. On screen was a "Cheers" re-run. "Dial don't never get turned off from 5."

Frank gave him the smile that launched a thousand Nielson wins. "That's great to hear."

"Everybody just like your style, Frank. Just figure it ain't the news less you give it."

Frank took a sip. "I appreciate that, Jackson. Were you watching tonight when that car blew up?"

"Oh, I seen it all right. Jesus, that poor woman and her kids."

"Yeah, you think you've seen everything in this town, and then there's this."

The bartender nodded. "You know the guy they lookin' for, the one that own the car? He come into the bar."

Frank put the beer down. "Tonight?"

"No, not tonight. I mean he been in here maybe five-six times."

The man with the skinny arms obviously wanted into this conversation and finally made his move. "I seen that bomb go too, Frank. Seen one go up in person down in Florida one time. Fuckin' awesome, man."

Unhappy with the interruption, Frank gave the man only a glance. "I'll bet." He asked Jackson, "So when was this guy in here last?"

Skinny Arms jumped in again. "You fuckin' bet. So, Frank, what's that Mary Scott bitch like? You ever lay the old sausage on her?"

Frank stared at the man: the eyes red-rimmed, the nose bent, the black hair thinning badly, the pallor distinctly unhealthy. The phrase "under a rock" came to mind. "Mary's a nice girl, and I'm happily married."

"Hey, what I hear, Frank, you fuck anything walks upright."

Frank smiled at the man, whose nose needed wiping. With a reasonably adept impersonation, he said: "Yeah, fuckin' awesome, man." Then he turned away. "So, Jackson, this Anthony Peoples who owned the car, when was he in here last?"

"Don't know, maybe two month ago. I only know him cause his cousin use to come in here all the time."

"Who's his cousin?"

"Guy named Richard Mahone. 'Pretty Rick' they called him. Also called him 'Maserati Rick' cause he like them Eye-talian cars. Say he was a roller. Big time."

"The same 'Maserati Rick' we did a story on recently?"

"Yeah, when they murdered his ass. Back a month or two, I

guess."

"And he was buried in a coffin made out of parts from his favorite vehicle. So who's 'they,' Jackson?"

"They?"

"Yeah, who murdered his ass?"

"Who knows?"

"Probably friends in the dope business?"

Jackson got busy wiping the bar and cocked his head. "Could be."

Skinny Arms barged in again: "Speaking of friends, Frank, one of yours did me a big ass favor a while back."

Frank decided the smile wouldn't work on this guy. "Yeah, I'll bet. Look, pal, I'm having an interesting conversation here with my friend Jackson, and you keep interrupting."

Skinny Arms dialed up to belligerent. "So I'm not interesting, eh, Frank? Well, fuck you, man. That friend a yours I was talkin' about? Happens to be his honor, Judge Bill J. O'Bryan."

Frank stared into the man's red eyes. "Bullshit."

"Yeah, bullshit, eh. Well, I caught a crack case a while back woulda put me away for 20 years, so I make a little charitable contribution to the judge through my lawyer, and poof! It all goes away."

With a long look at the guy's mouth, Frank decided there was a distinct resemblance to the rodent family. "So who's your attorney?"

The narrow, pale face puffed with rage. "Oh, so now you're interested, eh, Frank, you fuckin' phony! Let's see you tell that story on the fuckin' First at Five News."

"I don't tell bullshit stories, pal. Give me your attorney's name, and I'll check it out."

"Oh, sure you will, Frank, you fuckin' phony. He's another one of your fuckin' friends."

Suddenly animated, Jackson had moved around from behind the bar. Now he was all over the Rat Man, grabbing him by the back of the belt and the greasy hair over the nape of his neck. Yanked off the stool he squealed in pain, flailed his arms and kicked his feet as he was carried to the door.

"The man say don't interrupt. And I say haul your ass outta here and don't never bring it back. I ain't gonna be so fuckin' nice next time."

Tossed like a sack onto the street, the guy struggled to get himself upright. "Man, it's a free fuckin' country," he whined, then appeared to consider barging right back in. Finally, he thought better of it, stumbling off, then whirling with several obscene gestures.

Inside, Jackson headed back behind the bar. "Sorry about that asshole, Frank."

"No problem. Who is that guy?"

"Got me. His last time in here the same thing happen. Got soused and I run him out."

Chapter 9

He slipped in the key, and its soft raking sound filled the silent hallway. Opening the door with its usual squeak and ticking, he moved through the small foyer toward the murmuring movie voices coming from the living room TV. The still-lit candles were half-gone, the Chardonnay uncorked and one of the two glasses half-full. In the warm, scented room, she slept with her head back on the couch, her small pretty feet on the cocktail table, the short, sheer gown almost covering what it was supposed to.

He sat next to her and used the remote to silence Bogey and Bacall. Quietly pouring himself some wine, he took a long sip, then walked two fingers like a bug up one bare thigh.

Sherie stirred, and the blue eyes opened. "Oh, Frank, you scared me."

He gave her the smile. "You always say that, and you never sound scared. Besides, you said you like bugs. Most of them are harmless, you said, 'kinda cute.'"

She stared at the glowing VCR clock. "Yeah, I don't mind bugs. I just don't like some guy acting like a bug. One-fifteen, Frank. Where've you been?"

"Working."

"What do you mean, working?" She tugged at the hem of the shortie, trying to cover more with it than was ever intended.

"Working. I had to check out a lead."

"Frank, this was supposed to be our night."

"I know, sweetheart, I..."

"First, you cancel dinner. Then you don't show up until the middle of the night."

He put his glass down on the table, leaned forward and held the hand that was still tugging. "Calm down. Did you watch tonight?"

"Of course I watched. TV's the only time I get to see you these days."

"Sherie, cut it out. So you saw the car blow up with the mother and her kids."

She sighed and shook her head, meaning, yes, unfortunately she had.

"And you heard the guy with the camcorder?"

"Yeah, I saw that jerk."

"So in the break I ask the jerk if he knows where this guy Peoples hangs out. The guy who just lost his whole family. And he says he saw him once in a bar called Marvin's. So after the show I went there and found out this whole damn thing is probably drug-related."

She took her hand from his. "So, really. No shit. I could have told you that without going to the bar. Everything is drug-related. Ninety-five percent of all parking meter violations are drug-related."

He laughed. Occasionally the girl got off a good one, usually when she was angry. "Speaking of which, did you get my go-gos?"

She leaned back and closed her eyes, as if she were wondering what the hell she was doing with her life. "They're next to the TV."

Moving to the wall unit, he picked up the vial, rattled its contents and dropped it in a coat pocket. "So who's this doc who fills prescriptions without asking questions?"

"Forget it. You make your own connection, I'll never see you." The eyes were still closed.

Back at the couch, he sat even closer. "Baby, you know you drive me crazy."

"No, I know you *are* crazy. I have nothing to do with it."

"You look especially luscious in this sexy new thing."

She was still sulking but finally opened her big blues and let him take her in his arms. "I bought it just for you tonight."

"Well, I can't wait to see what it looks like tossed on a chair."

Kissing her softly, he knew from the way her beautiful head lolled back on his arm that everything would be just fine.

Chapter 10

The Sunday morning sun rose in a clear sky over the shimmering lake behind a large Bloomfield Hills home. At a fashionably distressed French farmhouse table, Marci, mid-40s in sweats, her dark blond hair in a clip, gazed at the sparkling water, looking for inspiration through the large picture window in her kitchen. She and 16-year-old Bobby, in jeans, a Nirvana "Nevermind" t-shirt and bare feet, were sharing the Free Press.

Her face still pretty but faded and settled, the woman gave up on inspiration and reached for the MinuteMaid. Bobby was lean and handsome, but his complexion was sallow, and his eyes were hooded at the moment.

"More juice, honey?"

A silent scowl at a folded-over page.

Still holding the carton: "Bobby, how about more juice?"

The boy finally looked up. "No thanks, Mom. You see Wil Barnes today?"

Marci put the carton down. "Reading Barnes is against my religion."

"He's got another thing in here about Dad."

"Why doesn't that surprise me?"

Bobby read aloud: "'The Sun King was jousting for the honor of his lady fair, or somebody's lady fair, Friday evening at the posh Black Knight Inn. Channel 5 eminence Frank DeFauw decked a young swain in the Knight's crowded dining room with a swift and surreptitious blow to the nether regions (a.k.a. a sucker punch to the gut). At the coveted Booth One the young stalwart had found his pretty blond favorite wedged between WTEM-TV's 'Frankie Franchise' and his long-time pal Recorder's Court Judge William O'Bryan. DeFauw, who has used his fists in more than one barroom encounter over the years, settled the matter quickly while his younger opponent was looking the other way. When asked by Your

Intrepid Reporter if that was his usual stratagem in physical encounters, the local Nielsen King would say only, 'Get away from me, you little (bleep).'"

The boy dropped the paper and stared at his mother.

Marci with a frown: "You had to spoil a perfectly lovely Sunday morning."

"Mom, you'd have seen it. One of your friends would have told you about it."

"No, I've got them trained not to."

"Why put up with his shit, Mom? Why not get a divorce? Or maybe an annulment. Ted's mother got an annulment. She said her husband never had any intention of keeping his vows, and the Pope granted an annulment."

"Sweetheart, I don't care about an annulment. One marriage has been more than enough."

Chapter 11

In a shiny black jogging suit Frank walked into the kitchen. "Well, what's this? Scheming a palace coup, are we?"

"Ah, the Sun King," said Bobby. "Wait'll you see Wil Barnes this morning."

Frank got himself coffee. "I saw it in last night's edition. As usual, the little prick got almost everything wrong."

"Like what?" The boy stared boldly at him.

Sitting at the table Frank faced his son. "Like she wasn't a blond. She was a brunette. And I didn't sucker punch the kid. I was just too fast for him."

Bobby was one large smirk.

"And Barnes never asked me if that was my usual M.O. He made that stuff up."

"Dad, you're so full of shit."

Marci finally looked up from the paper. "Bobby!"

Frank shook his head. "No, he's right. I am full of shit sometimes. Besides, it's good to see this boy show a little spunk for once. How about some golf this afternoon, kid? I'm playing with the Doctors Ross and Katz, and I could use a partner."

Bobby, on his feet: "No, thanks, I'm busy."

Annoyed, especially after handing the boy that "bullshit" business, Frank asked, "Busy doing what?"

"Homework."

"Homework! Do your damn homework instead of sitting up there all day in your room, jackin' off on that damn computer. Then you'd have time for some fun. The world is leaving you behind, Bobby boy."

Waving at Marci, the kid headed for the door. "Thanks for breakfast, Mom."

Frank tried to reel him back in. "Number one on the golf team this spring, and you quit. I hate to say I just see a quitter and a loser here."

Stopping in the doorway, Bobby said, "Yeah, you hate to say. And you say it all the time. Anyway, I didn't quit. My grades weren't good enough."

"With your brain, it amounts to the same thing. The only way you could fail is on purpose. Out of spite."

"Yeah, that's it. I'm spiting you. Later, Mom."

She called, "Bobby?" And when he walked off, not answering, she turned to Frank. "Why do you do that? You know what Dr. Fine said about calling him names."

He kept his angry voice low: "Look, Fine's had six months to show us something with this boy, and I've seen nothing. No improvement whatsoever. I try to reach out to him, ask him to play golf, something we always loved to do together when his brother was alive, and, no thanks, he'd rather sit in his damn room and do nothing."

She moved to the counter where she put two bran muffins on a plate. "You only ask when it's convenient. You've got your cronies along today, and he doesn't want to be around them."

"No, he just locks me out."

"Frank, do you realize…" She set the plate loudly in front of him. "…what it does to that boy to see something like that column in the paper today?"

"There's not a damn thing I can do about that. The guy's an asshole, and he's going to write what he wants no matter what I do."

"But you give him grist for his mill. It's the way you choose to live, and it's destructive to the people who are close to you and care about you. I know you think your daughter's doing just fine, but she's not. Jennie's drinking too much and, I think she's way too adventurous, let's say, with way too many young men. She's got real problems, Frank."

"Oh, bullshit." He caught the echo of his son's earlier response.

"Your capacity for denial, Frank, is unbelievable."

"Yeah, well, it doesn't help these kids to hear you talk about divorce."

"I never talk about it. In front of them."

"Well, maybe just annulment."

She was up from the table. "Bobby brought that up. He's only trying to protect me."

"From what?"

"From you, Frank. I'm really beginning to think divorce *is* the only answer."

Trailing an angry exhaust, Marci stalked out. Frank shook his head, picked up a bran muffin, then dropped it back on the plate. With his coffee mug he headed for the kitchen's back door, open on a large deck.

Walking out, he moved past the expensive outdoor furniture to the far end of the deck. He stared at the quiet, sunny lake. A lone seagull rode the bow of the speedboat moored at their small dock.

Often when feeling down, or maybe in the grasp of something robbing his control, he would craft a small game with fate. So, if the gull stayed in place for at least the next five seconds, everything would be okay. Starting his slow, even count, he got as far as three.

Chapter 12

From the bench in his blond-paneled courtroom in the Frank Murphy Hall of Justice came the stern voice of Judge William O'Bryan.

"And it is the determination of this court that you be sentenced to..."

A TV cameraman rolled on the proceedings from one corner. In front of Judge O'Bryan at the bench were the court reporter, her fingers flashing as she stabbed her machine, and the uniformed bailiff, a lean competent looking man with a large, irregular strawberry birthmark covering the left side of his face. Standing in front of them, the girlish prosecutor and the portly defense attorney, sporting red suspenders, were both looking at the defendant, a well-built young guy with the hint of a smile and his short-sleeves rolled up even shorter to show off the full glory of his extensively tattooed arms.

"...not less than 12 years," said the judge, staring hard at the defendant, "and not more than 20 years at the State Department of Corrections facility at Jackson. This court feels strongly..."

Suddenly the defendant leapt forward, lunged past the court reporter and was almost instantly at the judge's throat. He was screaming, "You motherfuckin' pig! I'll rip your fuckin' head off!"

Moving quickly, the bailiff grabbed the defendant's ample head of hair and promptly yanked him off the judge. Then with one arm around the defendant's neck and the other clamping his colorful right arm behind his back, the bailiff restored order.

Chapter 13

"An unusual outburst today in the courtroom of Recorder's Court Judge William O'Bryan..."

While Mary Scott fiddled with one of her bracelets, Frank read from the page in front of him, occasionally glancing at a small monitor built into the anchor desk. On the monitor was that surprising scene captured earlier by the TV camera in the courtroom.

"Melvin Street, convicted last month of armed robbery in the hold-up of a bank on the city's eastside, listened as the judge sentenced him to prison for 12-to-20 years. And then, as you'll see, Mr. Street went berserk."

Frank watched the monitor now and listened to the judge say: "This court feels strongly that..."

Then Street made his move. "You (--bleep--), I'll rip your (--bleep--) head off!"

Frank continued his narration: "Mr. Street was quickly subdued and ushered out of the courtroom." Looking up now, he smoothly transitioned to the teleprompter: "He was returned later in shackles to hear the rest of what Judge O'Bryan had to say, with no further incident."

Frank paused for a second, then began again. "Police today are still looking for the man whose wife and two children were killed in a car bombing last Friday in front of the family's home on the city's westside. Thirty-two-year-old Anthony Peoples may have been the bomb's intended victim..."

Chapter 14

In a cramped, shabby room without windows, a thin black man was lying very still on a bare mattress and watching a small fuzzy TV picture of Frank speaking to the camera.

"But police are saying little about the case—only that they think Mr. Peoples was not in the home at the time of the blast and that they want to talk with him."

As the screen showed a still-frame of a car engulfed in flames, the man on the bed closed his eyes but opened them again as Frank continued.

"This reporter, however, has learned that the bombing, which took the lives of 31-year-old Juanita Peoples and her two children, five-year-old Damon and three-year-old Sara, may have been drug-related."

On the TV now was a picture of a woman and two children in a formal pose, and the man glanced at a plastic three-legged stool next to the bed, holding a small, shade-less lamp, a wallet-sized photo that matched the TV picture and a rip-edged newspaper clipping folded so that it showed half the face of columnist Wil Barnes.

Chapter 15

In the large, brightly lit studio at WTEM with huge cityscape photographs made to look like windows, Frank gazed straight at a camera and read.

"According to our information, Mr. Peoples is the cousin of this man, Richard 'Pretty Rick' Mahone, who was reputed to be one of this area's major narcotics dealers. Mahone, also known as 'Maserati Rick,' was murdered two months ago. And, while police refuse to confirm or deny any of this, the bombing may be part of an on-going turf war between rival drug gangs."

Frank turned to Mary, who was about to start reading, and began ad-libbing. "You know, Mary, maybe we at Channel 5 can be of some help in resolving this situation..."

In the darkened control room, flanked by Dennis Clark and the switcher, the director stared at the glowing bank of monitors and threw up his hands. "What the hell's he doing?"

Dennis: "It's okay. Just stay with him!"

"...Mr. Peoples, if you or anyone who can reach you are watching this newscast, I will meet with you anywhere, anytime, so that you can be certain your story is fully and accurately told and your personal safety insured."

The director: "Is he nuts!?"

Dennis: "Maybe, but he's also a genius."

"This guy Peoples could be a maniac. Maybe *he* did his wife and kids."

"Don't worry, the guy'll never call. But our ratings'll jump two points for the next month."

In the studio Frank's heavily made up face appeared genuinely concerned and earnest. "If at some point you want me to arrange a meeting with any law enforcement agency in this city, I will do that in a way that will offer you maximum protection. In any case, Mr. Peoples, give me a call here at the station, name your time and place, and I'll be there."

He turned to his smoldering co-anchor. "Mary?"

Staring wide-eyed at Frank, she glanced down at her script, then up at a camera. "Frank, in a surprise move today Wayne County prosecutor Prentis Gant resigned his post effective immediately."

Watching his desk monitor, Frank checked out the good-looking black man speaking at a podium.

Mary continued: "At a news conference this morning, the 38-year-old Gant said he was leaving only a year and a half after being elected to the job for what he called personal and family reasons."

Gant's voice filled the studio: "I'll be entering private practice, but I hope to remain active in this community and to serve its needs, perhaps in some other capacity."

On Frank's monitor the screen showed a short, rotund man in his late 40s appearing at the podium, as Mary read, "Gant will be replaced by long-time assistant prosecutor Peter Canzoneri, who's been with the county prosecutor's office for the past twenty-three years. Canzoneri will serve in the post until the elections this November."

Chapter 16

"And the press in this town, especially the columnists at our papers, where, of course, they do news way more legit than TV, went nuts with this story."

Under a banner that proclaimed "The Economic Club of Detroit" and flanked by the mayor and other pols on one side and the suits who ran the club on the other, Frank was speaking to a large luncheon audience. He paused at the podium, his eyes closed for a moment, a gesture of vulnerability that some in the huge room thought calculated but that others were sure was pure instinct with Frank.

"Had Tommy been drinking at the time? Was he an alcoholic? Did he have a substance abuse problem? Was he toking a joint out there in the boat? All of it without the slightest foundation in fact. And there was nothing we could do to preserve my son's memory and set the record straight. So, yes, of course I'm acutely aware of the abuses in this business."

At a table near the podium, he glimpsed an attractive redhead pulling a ballpoint pen and a pad of yellow sticky notes from her purse. She scribbled something as he continued:

"And certainly not all of us exercise the responsibility that goes with the privilege of having such a powerful voice."

At the same table, a fellow he occasionally employed as an attorney leaned to the ear of the guy next to him with what could be either a frown or a smile. Frank imagined the whispered message: "Look who's talking."

Frank's voice was ringing now: "Maybe, you say there should be some way to curb or disallow this kind of excess? Some way to insure that we'll all be a little more civil and considerate to each other. And I say..."

A slight pause, again for dramatic effect. "...absolutely not. The vital importance of the First Amendment is inviolable. The right to speak and publish freely is clearly indispensable to a democratic society. Let me just leave you with one brief quote."

The attorney leaned to his seatmate again, and this time Frank could almost read his lips: "Here comes 'good old Jimmy Madison.'"

Frank said, "James Madison, fourth president of the United States, also known as the 'Father of the Constitution.' Here's what old Jimmy Madison said about freedom of the press, and I'm quoting: 'Knowledge will forever govern ignorance. And a people who mean to be their own governors, must arm themselves with the power knowledge gives. A popular government without popular information or the means of acquiring it, is but a prologue to a farce or a tragedy, or perhaps both.'"

Pausing one last time, he let the thought sink deeper before waving goodbye. "Thanks so much for inviting me. I enjoyed it."

Applause rose as the redhead and many others around her stood. Frank nodded and waved again, then moved from the podium, pausing briefly to shake hands with the mayor. As a suit took the microphone, the redhead embarked for the steps Frank would use to come down from the dais.

"That's it folks," said the suit. "We're running late, so thanks to Frank for his inspiration, and we'll see you all next week."

As Frank descended the steps, the woman put her hand on his arm. "Hi, Frank, I'm Letty Pell."

"Well, hello, Letty Pell. I love your name." His smile said he also liked the rest of Letty.

"Well, I loved your speech, and I'd love to see you sometime to further discuss all the important things you talked about today." She pressed the yellow sticky note into the palm of his hand. "Here's my number. I'll be waiting for your call."

Then, after offering a mischievous smile, Letty leaned close to say softly, "And I give incredible head."

He glanced at his hand and then at her perfect smiling mouth. "Well, thanks, Letty. It's so nice to meet you."

Letty with a wink: "Call me."

As Frank moved with the rest of the crowd toward the exits, the attorney put an arm around his shoulder.

"What'd she say, Frank?"

"She says she gives great head."

"You bullshitter."

"I swear to god, Jimmy. I love these liberated women."

Jim Goodman nodded with a smile. "Hey, enough with James Madison."

"So you're my attorney, and you've heard it too many times. Most people haven't. By the way, Jimmy, what do you hear about this city's august Recorder's Court? We got any judges whose palms might be greased?"

"Oh, I've heard stories..."

"About whom?"

"Frank, it's just rumor and hearsay."

"Judge Billy?"

"O'Bryan?" Jim Goodman smiled and shrugged in a way that could mean yes or no.

Chapter 17

The newsroom was quiet, almost empty after the newscast. Francine Rickey sat in front of a TV set watching Dan Rather while eating a sandwich. When Frank strolled through with a light step reflecting a good mood, he spoke in a dead-on imitation of Rather. "Francine...Good work today."

The startled young woman seemed uncertain whether Frank was serious. "Oh, hi, Frank. You were great."

He swapped the Rather bit for mock conceit. "Frankie, truthfully I'm always great. But seriously your writing today was excellent. Sharp, crisp, evocative yet always to the point. And that kicker about the two-headed dog had some real wit to it."

Francine was nearly speechless. "Ah, I really, ah, appreciate that, Frank."

"Hey, keep up the great work. But why are you sitting here all alone eating out of a bag? Why aren't you out with your boyfriend having a real dinner?"

She put the sandwich down, half-embarrassed. "I don't have a boyfriend."

"Oh, I can't believe that. Great lookin' gal like you."

Francine picked up her sandwich again. "It's sad but true, Frank."

Grinning, Frank moved on. "Well, I'll tell you what, Frankie. My wife ever keeps her promise and divorces me? I'll marry you. How's that sound?"

Francine smiled wryly. "Sounds great, Frank."

Chapter 18

There was still good daylight left on this balmy evening when he spotted Letty Pell waiting on Washington Boulevard in front of an office building. In the red Viper with the top down Frank stopped in front of her.

"Hey, how about a lift, gorgeous?"

With a lusty smile, Letty slipped into the seat next to Frank. "I'm so pleased you called." As if they were old lovers, she moved close and gave him a long, warm kiss on the mouth.

When she finished, he was already stirred. "Gees, you are one friendly girl."

Letty dropped her eyes and then a hand to his warm lap. "Oh, my, we'll have to do something about this very soon."

"We will?"

"Oh, you bet. I've been thinking about this all afternoon."

An angry horn came from a car behind. They looked around to find the driver with his hands up off the wheel, mouthing something unpleasant. Frank laughed and drove off.

Letty asked, "Where we going?"

"Little place I know. Nothing special, but it's quiet and kinda charming."

With her hand in his lap again: "Sounds romantic."

As Frank moved the convertible through medium traffic on Michigan Avenue, other motorists could see Letty's pretty red head disappear into Frank's lap, and then bob up again with a smile and a laugh. The best view was from the cab of a furniture delivery truck moving up in the lane next to the Viper. From the truck's raised cab both the driver and his partner were watching with considerable interest.

The driver finally gave them a blast on the horn, and the other guy rolled down his window and yelled, "Hey, ain't that you, Frank?"

Letty bobbed up, and Frank glanced back and shook his head.

"Hell, yes, it's you. Hey, man, how's she doin'?"

His head back with a laugh, Frank gunned the Viper ahead.

Letty giggled. "You always attract so much attention?"

Frank shrugged. "Comes with the job. At least with a gorgeous red head in the car."

Chapter 19

Though the hour was earlier this time, at Marvin's Bar there was only a sparse crowd. Jackson was again behind the bar, and Myra, an overweight waitress with a limp, took her good, sweet time serving two booths and a table. When Frank and Letty entered looking wind-blown, they headed for an empty booth half-way back.

Letty was obviously trying to spot the place's charm as Frank called out, "Jackson, how you doin'?"

"Okay, Frank. We seen you tonight, and I was tellin' everybody you was in here. Nobody believe it."

"You want an autographed photo to put over the bar? That way they'll have to believe."

"That would be good, Frank. Thanks."

Letty slid into the booth as Frank said, "No problem, man. You know, I've been telling the lady here that Marvin's has the best burgers in town."

"They ain't that good, miss. But if you're hungry, we can probably take care of you."

Frank sat across from Letty. "Jackson here is the world's last honest man."

Letty took Frank's hand. "Well, Jackson, you have a charming little place here."

"Well, that ain't true neither, ma'am, but we thank you for sayin' it."

Letty laughed, and by now Myra had limped up to the booth.

"Hello, I'm Myra, and I'll be your server this evening."

Frank chuckled. "Hey, Myra. We'll each have a burger deluxe, and I'll have a Bud Lite."

Letty said, "Me too."

"You too what?" snarled Myra.

Letty laughed again, this time a lusty peal. "I'll have a Bud Lite."

Limping off Myra screamed, "Two Bud Lites!"

Frank said, "I told you, they treat me like royalty in here."

Jackson had moved around from behind the bar to the booth. "Frank, that guy I run outta here when you was here before?"

"Yeah?"

"Name is Byrd. Randal Byrd."

"Bird, as in cuckoo?"

"Yeah, Byrd with a Y."

"Randal Byrd, B-Y-R-D."

"Right. He come in again and I carded him. Said he don't look 21."

"How'd he take it?"

Jackson was heading back behind the bar again. "He was pissed. But he wanted a drink more than he didn't want to be carded."

With Frank and Jackson talking, a bearded, heavy-set fellow had moved from the back of the bar and was standing now directly in front of Frank. He was wearing a T-shirt that strained to contain his belly. The shirt said, "I Like Tits."

Frank looked up, read the shirt and said, "Can I help you, pal?"

"Yeah, Frank, you could retire."

"Retire, eh?"

"Yeah, man, then I wouldn't have to watch your fuckin' face on TV."

Frank glanced at Letty, telling her with a brow lift that he'd been through this a million times. Then he said, "You know, I didn't catch your name."

"Name's Merle."

"Well, Merle, why not turn the dial?"

Merle smirked and swayed, glancing back at his two buddies watching avidly at the pool table. "I don't have to turn the fuckin' dial. I don't never watch your ass anyways."

"Then what's the problem?"

"The problem? I'll tell you what the problem is. You, Frank. You're the fuckin' problem. You don't never give just the straight news like people want. You always gotta put your fuckin' two cents worth in. And that's about all it's worth, is two cents."

"So you'd like a little more journalistic objectivity."

"No, I'd like a lot less Frank on TV."

"Well, Merle, but how do you know all this if you never watch me?"

"See, right there, that's your problem. You're a smart ass. I don't have to watch you. Everybody knows this shit. Like tonight talkin' about that car bomb like you know all this stuff, like it's drug-related, and you don't know shit."

Frank's tone remained reasonable and friendly. "So, Merle, you know something about it?"

"I don't know nothin' about it. But I'm not on TV like you, actin' like I do."

Behind Merle Frank spotted Randal Byrd walking into the bar. Byrd saw Frank at about the same time, and their eyes locked. After a second Frank called out: "Hey, Randal Byrd, let's talk."

Byrd froze for an instant, glanced at Jackson, then wheeled out of the bar. Quickly on his feet, Frank did a brief dance with Merle, then sprinted for the door.

Crossing the dark street in front of the bar, Byrd ran hard, spinning around a car that nearly hit him as it screeched to a halt. As Frank reached the street, Byrd was disappearing into an alley on the other side. Dodging traffic, Frank followed, but when he finally entered the alley, there was no sign of Byrd.

Back inside the bar, he found Jackson sitting with Letty. Obviously in Frank's absence the bartender had carefully outlined Merle's options for him. When Frank passed his table, the man who loved tits barely gave him a glance.

Jackson struggled out of the booth as Frank arrived. "Any luck, Frank?"

"Naw, must have slithered down some rat hole."

"Who was that?" asked Letty without a smile now.

Frank looked up suddenly feeling weary. "Oh, just a little rodent who gave me trouble the last time in here."

"Well, you look exhausted. We need to eat our burgers and find a place for you to lie down." She tilted her head and gave him a wink.

Giving her one back, he nodded. "Yeah, I was up at six this morning, writing." He slipped his vial of little reds out of his breast pocket, popped one out and swallowed it. "You want a little extra energy?"

She smiled and shook her head. He swallowed some beer and put the pills away, knowing that he'd be quietly boasting in a few seconds. There was clearly no need to with this gal. So was he that insecure, or did he just want an excuse in case his performance later was less than sterling?

"Up at six! What are you writing?" She was already impressed.

He blew smoke at the dingy ceiling. "Oh, it's a labor of love, mostly. I'm writing a history of the small Belgian community in this city. Probably about four people outside my family will read it, but I've been interviewing folks of my grandfather's and father's generations for a couple years now, and I'm telling their tales."

He brightened as he talked about this, as he usually did. "Really, their stories are incredible, the ones who came just after the turn of the century. Like my grandfather who arrived from Antwerp at the age of 16 with a buck and a quarter in his pocket. Unbelievable what they went through and how they made it."

Letty took his hand in both of hers. "Well, you've already got me hooked. I'll be reader number five."

Chapter 20

On a gorgeous Sunday evening Frank leaned against a wood piling on his dock next to the speedboat and stared at the big orange sun setting over the mirror-like lake. The familiar whine and slap of the screen door at the back of the house called to him, and he turned to find his 19-year-old daughter walking across the large deck. Jennie waved, smiled and moved down the steps to a lawn that sloped gracefully to the lake. She was a pretty blond with a cute figure in her shorts-over-leotard, and she moved with her mother's sly swing of the hips.

"Hi, Daddy."

"Hello, baby."

Nestling to him, she kissed him on the cheek. "How's my favorite dad?"

He puts his arms around her, then leaned back to look into her narrowed blue eyes. "I'm fine, sweetie, how about you?"

"Fine."

"Little hung over this morning? You seemed a tad under the weather."

"Oh, maybe just a little. But I ran it off."

"Keep 'em little, and you'll be fine."

Jennie frowned and pushed lightly away from him. "God, Daddy, don't *you* start on me."

"Start what?"

"Oh, Mom's been on my case like crazy."

"About?"

"About drinking and carousing—just normal stuff."

Frank gave her a shocked look. "You're carousing?"

She gave him a small smile. "A little."

"Honey, you know your mom. She's just a worry-wart who loves you to pieces." He took her hand, and together they walked down the dock. At the end they stood and gazed at the sun's perfect reflection on the lake.

Always the touchy-feely one in the family, Jennie snuggled up to him again and spoke softly: "What was all the yelling about?"

"We weren't yelling. Just our usual domestic banter, with your mother threatening divorce."

"She's doing that again?"

"She never stopped."

"I thought maybe it was because of what day it is."

"What day is it?"

"You know, Daddy. A year to the day since the accident."

Frank's arm around her spare, sweet shoulders squeezed her even closer to him. "I know, baby. We just have to put it behind us. Life goes on. Because it has to."

"Daddy, you always say that. But a day hasn't gone by that I haven't thought about Tommy and what happened."

"Honey, I hope to Christ you're not still blaming yourself. You promised me you wouldn't do that."

The girl moved away from him to the edge of the dock and stared down at the water just barely moving at the pilings. "Yeah, I know. But how can I not blame myself?"

"Because it was an accident, baby. If anyone was to blame it was Tommy himself. But it was simply an accident."

When she spoke again, it was with a thin quiver of her lip. "Okay, so Tommy had too much beer, but so did I. No, he shouldn't have been hot-dogging, backwards on that ski. But I shouldn't have been driving so fast. Yes, it was just bloody fate or whatever that the Fisher's dog was swimming out there, and I veered to avoid him. But if I had been under better control, it just would not have happened."

Frank moved up to hold his daughter's shoulders and stop their shiver. "Baby, you're way too hard on yourself."

Jennie didn't answer and stared up at the sun hanging huge above the tree line across the lake. Then her gaze moved down and to the right to the remnants of an ancient dock in the water in front of a home about half-mile away. After a long pause she said, "You know, sometimes I wish they had left that damn piling sticking up out there in front of the Fisher place. Because for me, every time I look out there, I still see it. I know exactly where it was. I see it right now, even though I watched them pull it out with that crane. How long am I going to still see it out there? Probably for the rest of my life. I

44

have dreams about it, weird nightmares, really. It's gone for a while and then one day it's back again, all bloody. Once, in one dream, I even took your chain saw out there and started chopping it off at the waterline, and it starting talking to me, screaming at me, telling me it was alive and I was killing it."

He squeezed her softly and kissed the crown of her head. "I'm so sorry, baby. I had no idea."

She turned to him, tears on her cheeks. "No, how could you know? I haven't talked to anybody about it."

While Jennie tucked herself into her father's arms, her head on his chest, he held her, and, not trusting his own voice, said nothing. Without a question or a doubt, he had always felt he would give his life for his kids, and yet, with this sweet grieving girl, he'd been deaf, dumb and blind.

Chapter 21

At one end of the quiet newsroom, in the lazy pause after lunch and before the afternoon's editorial meeting, Dennis Clark half-sat on the edge of a desk where Blanche Barowski, the news director's heavy-set secretary, held up a garish greeting card, homemade with gold script and multicolor ink sketches.

"Look at this one," said the perpetually red-faced Blanche, who also handled Frank's correspondence. "Hand-printed with a long poem called 'Jesus and Frank.'"

She handed him the card, and he opened it like an accordion.

"Good Christ! This must have taken weeks."

Then Dennis read aloud: "'Jesus and Frank are my two best friends. For the sins of the world they make amends. When the news was bad and our hearts sank, who did we turn to but Jesus and Frank?'"

He laughed with a sad delight. "This is incredible."

"You wouldn't believe the stuff he gets." Blanche pointed to a large box on the corner of the desk. "Holy cards, novena cards, home remedies. They all have the answer to his backaches and his headaches and every other malady they imagine he has. This is just from the last few days." She picked up a large wad of letters and dropped them into the box.

"You give it all to him?"

"All except the hate mail, the really vicious stuff, and he gets a lot of that too."

"Well, that's his secret. You either love him or hate him. Nobody's neutral. You see the paper today?"

"No."

"Wil Barnes' column." Dennis grabbed a section of the paper from a nearby desk.

Blanche rolled her eyes. "Again?"

"It's a blind item, but it's obvious who he's talking about. Here it is. 'Strange Sighting Department: Was that who we think it was? Our favorite TV journalist (How's that for an oxymoron, folks?) tooling through a downtown avenue in his fancy flivver with a drop-dead redhead (not his wife) often dipping from view?'"

"What's an oxymoron?"

"It's a contradiction in terms. Like TV journalist. Get it?"

"Got it. That should be worth another fifty irate letters."

"So where is our favorite oxymoron?"

"In with the boss."

Chapter 22

"Frank, you were in a convertible." Alice Whitney sat with a cup of tea at one end of a couch. Frank was next to her in an armchair. A handsome woman in her 50s, Alice wore her VP-GM suit with just a hint of cleavage, her fashion reflecting her manner: firm but feminine.

"So? Lots of people have convertibles."

"Not like yours."

"Alice, I didn't know she'd do that."

"You knew exactly what she'd do."

"Women throw themselves at me, Alice. I can't help it. I'm irresistible." This was delivered with the kind of practiced self-mockery that usually got her to drop the whole thing.

"Frank, to coin a phrase, just say no. Especially when we're in a book, and you're in a convertible."

"Jesus, Alice, let me have some fun. We're nearly out of May and the numbers are fine. We're going to win again, for what, the 15th book in a row?"

"Don't kid yourself, Frank, the audience is restless out there. They're doing a lot of sampling. And we're down a half point in the last two weeks. Look, all I'm saying, Frank, is this is a pretty conservative town. You know that better than I do. You grew up here. And you know how many Catholics there are. They'll accept a little booze, and they may even accept a little wenching. But they won't accept wenching in public, and neither will I."

"How about in private, just you and me?"

Alice smiled sadly and ignored him. "How's your back these days?"

"I'm sure we could find a position that wouldn't put too much stress on it."

They had been through this kind of scene a million times, and she was still smiling and ignoring him. "How about the headaches?"

"I'd never have one with you."

"Frank, just stay out of his column. That's all I'm asking."

Chapter 23

The hollow, echoing smack of the hard rubber ball careening off the front wall was followed by the distinctly middle-aged grunts coming from Frank and Judge O'Bryan. Both men were shirtless and sweating as they flew around the court, jostling and bumping each other in a frantic effort to win this final point. When Frank dove and missed the shot to lose the match he pounded his racket on the floor and screamed, "You tripped me, you son of a bitch!"

The judge screamed back, "You tripped yourself!" Gasping and out of breath, they were both obviously exaggerating their anger.

"You cheat your ass off."

"Whatever it takes, man."

"You admit it!"

"I admit nothing," said the judge. "I'm simply stating a basic philosophical principle."

Heading through a door in the court's back wall into the racquetball lounge, each grabbed a towel from a nearby chair and mopped his sweaty face. Two attractive young women were there waiting for the court.

"So you tripped me on philosophical grounds?"

Frank noted the women, and said, "Hi, girls."

In mocking unison the women called out, "Hi, boys," then walked into the court without looking back. Frank checked them out over his shoulder as he and the judge headed for the locker room.

"Boys?" said Frank.

"They were putting you down, Frank."

"Me? What about you?"

"You called them 'girls.'"

"I hate liberated women."

"You have to know how to handle them."

Frank pushed through the locker room door and headed for a line of lockers and benches. He looked around to find the room unoccupied.

"Big talk. How's your physics major?"

"Who?"

"You know, the blond. What was her name? Kim? Kim the Bim."

"Oh, yeah, I have a new one. She's into space medicine."

Arriving at their lockers they sat on benches and removed their shoes and socks. Frank asked, "By the way, how was that guy's body odor the other day?"

"What?"

"The guy who tried to choke you. When we ran that tape the other night, I figured the boy probably had a bad case of B.O."

"I couldn't tell you. He was choking me so hard I couldn't breathe."

"So why'd he go off like that?"

"Well, I had just taken the prime of his youth and shoved it in the can for the next ten or fifteen years. It's not hard to understand."

Frank slipped off his shorts and jockstrap. "But most of those slimeballs don't jump you when you send them away."

Naked now the two men were walking to the shower, each carrying a towel to place on a hook just outside the shower room. Inside they found two other fellows, just finishing, who left the water running. Frank and the judge moved under the steamy spray.

"They'd all love to strangle me," said the judge when they were alone. "I'm not exactly popular with that group."

Frank let the water hit him in the face with his eyes closed. "You are very popular with a guy I met recently."

"Oh, yeah?"

"Yeah, a sleezoid character I ran into in a dive a couple weeks ago. Said you could have put him away for 20 years. But instead you worked out some kind of a deal and let him walk."

The judge turned his back to Frank and faced the spray. "Yeah? What kind of a deal?"

"A bribe is the term I think he used."

The judge turned to meet Frank's gaze, but when he answered there was no discernable change in his casual, almost bored tone. "A bribe, eh? That's another of my occupational hazards."

"What, taking bribes?"

"No, having scumbags running around saying they made this, that or the other deal with me. I put so many shitheads away and ruin so many plans to continue cheating and stealing and killing, it's a wonder it doesn't happen more often."

"So, you don't take bribes?"

"How much did this asshole say I took?"

"He didn't."

"Did you get his name?"

"Byrd. B-Y-R-D. Randal Byrd.

The judge paused for a moment, apparently searching his memory. "Doesn't ring a bell. Did he say who his attorney was?"

"No."

"That's another thing that happens. Some of these boys who've worked the court a while will tell their client, 'Look, I can get your case before Judge So-And-So, and for a $50,000 contribution, or whatever, he'll throw out your case.' And all along they know it'll be tossed anyway, or has been already because of some technicality."

"And then they pocket the 50 grand."

"It's easy to justify. Here you got the scum of the earth with millions stashed from rollin' dope or whatever. Is he going to miss a little 50 thou contribution to your kid's college fund?"

"Whatever it takes, man."

"What?"

Frank smiled. "Just stating a basic philosophical principle."

Chapter 24

In a gilded frame the photograph showed a young man in his late teens with casual good looks. His sandy hair tossed by a gust of wind, he offered a careless grin to someone unseen, the moment caught candidly on the deck with the sun and the lake doing a million twinkles in the background.

Frank was holding the frame and staring at this picture in the young man's still-intact bedroom with photos of sports stars and athletic teams covering one wall and on another, floor-to-ceiling bookshelves the boy had built himself with bricks and boards, still loaded with all of his books, an impressive array worthy of a young Renaissance type.

So why, staring at 18-year-old Tom, soon off to his first year at U. of M., did Frank's mind leap back to 4-year-old Tommy? To the day he had brought the boy with him to the library, as he so often had in those days, to use the dime-a-copy duplicating machine, to copy the manuscript pages he was churning out for a novel he never finished. A kind of ritual for father and son, the other kids being too young to drag along at the time. Put the page print-side down on the glass, close the cover, plunk in the dime and hear the machine whirl as the green light gleamed at the edges of its scan. The little kid with the big eyes had pressed himself against the machine and watched carefully as the emerging copies had stacked themselves on the side.

On this particular day, needing also the contents of a short chapter in a book on World War II Belgium, he had brought it to the copier with little Tommy trailing behind. Having promised Marci he'd be back for dinner in a half-hour, he had hurried to open the book to the right page and place it on the glass.

Next to him the boy's little voice had been urgent. "But, Daddy, wait! What...?"

He had given the child a few seconds to find his question, but it hadn't come. "Just wait, kiddo. I'll talk to you about it in the car."

Later in the Bonneville he had asked over his shoulder about the question.

What would happen, the little boy had asked, if you didn't put anything under the machine's cover and then put in your dime?

Well, he said, the machine would give you just a plain white sheet of paper.

Tommy had thought about that for a while and then asked: "What would happen if you put a crayon on the glass and covered it up?"

Still not sure where this was heading, he had said, "I guess the machine would give you a piece of paper with a little blotch on it the size and shape of the crayon."

More silence and then he had finally understood the boy's dilemma. "You thought," he had said, glancing at those brown eyes in the rearview mirror, "that the copying machine really was a copying machine, didn't you? You thought if you put in a book or a crayon, the machine would make you another book or a crayon."

"Yes," the boy had said, looking sheepishly away from the mirror.

"Yes, wouldn't it be great if the machine really did that?"

"Yes." Tommy had brightened with a smile.

Of course he'd gone on to explain how the machine really worked, by "taking a picture" of whatever you put on the glass. But he had silently reveled in the thought that his son might well be a budding scientist, formulating his little hypotheticals, then assessing his outcomes in an effort to explain his world.

Yes, the boy had grown into a sensitive, articulate young man, a graceful athlete with a marvelous mind and a keen, off-beat sense of humor. His siblings, friends, teachers and adoring parents were all expecting special things from him until...

With his back to the room's open door, he heard a soft shuffle behind him. He turned and found Bobby walking past in the hallway. His son stopped and looked in.

The two exchanged glances, but Frank, still lost in his reverie, said nothing, then looked back at the photograph. After a few seconds Bobby shook his head and left. Frank looked back again, this time to the empty doorway.

"Bobby?"

There was no answer, and Frank returned his gaze to the picture in his hand, wondering what it was about this younger boy that made him impossible to talk to.

Chapter 25

"Fabulous chow."

"Thanks so much for having us."

"Our pleasure, thanks for being had!"

In a two-story foyer with a cathedral ceiling and circular staircase Judge William O'Bryan and wife Gloria were saying goodbye to Frank and Marci DeFauw and two other couples. But the scene was stopped by the entrance at the top of the stairs of an exquisite four-year-old in a pink nightie. Missy O'Bryan was dragging a well-worn blue blanket in one hand and carrying "Green Eggs and Ham" in the other as she slowly descended the staircase.

"Daddy, I need you."

There was warm laughter and various adoring noises.

The judge literally glowed as he turned to his daughter. "You need me, darling? It's the middle of the night, sweetheart."

Missy sat on the stairs half-way down. "I need you, Daddy, to read me this book."

More adoring noises.

"Baby, we just read "Green Eggs" a few hours ago, before you went to sleep."

"Daddy, I NEED you!"

Clearly the judge had no choice. He kissed Marci, who was standing in front of him, and waved to the others. "Sorry, folks, I am needed! Thanks so much for coming."

A chorus of "Our pleasure," "Go ahead!" and "Take care of that little girl," accompanied the judge on the staircase as he scooped up his daughter and carried her to the second floor. His wife kissed Frank and then Marci and said, "Our little love child has daddy wrapped."

Frank said, "He never could resist a beautiful girl."

Gloria rolled her eyes with an exasperated flair. "Yeah, tell me about it."

Marci whispered, "It was wonderful, Glo. I'll call you."

Gloria squeezed her hand one last time. "Great. Thanks for being so sweet."

Frank and Marci moved out the front door. After a few steps he turned to glance at the judge's large home, its elaborate array of windows in the foyer lit up impressively against the night sky. They walked together in silence to the Viper parked at the end of the long circular drive.

With the remote he snapped open the locks on both doors and said, "Maybe that's what we should do."

"What?"

"Have a little love child of our own."

Her voice turned both angry and amused. "Frank, you are truly nuts."

"Nuts?"

"Yeah, nuts. We passed that point years ago."

They slid into the car and closed their doors. With a calm, reasonable tone, he said, "Gloria was forty when she had Missy."

"Well, I'm forty-three, and my child-bearing years are long gone. Period."

He started the Viper and flicked on its headlights.

She followed up: "Besides, even if I were younger, I wouldn't have another child with you."

"Why?" He moved the car forward slowly into the night.

"Because of the way you've been acting as a husband and a father for longer than I care to remember."

"Christ, let's not start that again."

"Good idea."

They drove in silence for a while. Finally, he said, "Tell me something. You've known Billy as long as I have, right?"

"Almost. I met him at that freshman tea dance he claims not to remember."

"All right, so tell me this. Is Billy O'Bryan capable of taking a bribe?"

Marci turned in her seat to look at him. "A bribe? Like in exchange for keeping somebody out of jail or something?"

"Yeah, that would be a bribe."

"Uhmm...sure, I think so."

"Really. I'm amazed you say that so easily."

"Why? There's always been something unscrupulous about Billy."

"Unscrupulous? You're just saying that because you think he's a womanizer."

"I *know* he's a womanizer. But that has nothing to do with it."

"What do you mean, you *know* he's a womanizer? Has he ever come on to you?"

"No comment."

"No comment! That means he has."

"No, it means no comment. It means I have absolutely no intention of talking to you about who has or has not come on to me, and what, if anything, I've done about it. Not with someone with your track record, Frank. Besides, as I said, it has nothing to do with why I think he'd take a bribe."

He decided the track record conversation should be avoided at the moment. "So why then?"

"Because Billy's greedy. And lazy. And capable of rationalizing almost anything."

He shook his head. "Jesus, I always thought you liked him."

"I do. But none of us is perfect. You should hear what I really think of you."

Chapter 26

Mid-afternoon was always the busiest time in the newsroom. In his shirt-sleeves Frank was pounding away at a computer keyboard as if it were an old-fashioned manual. Francine walked up and handed him a sheet of paper.

"Frank, here's the info you wanted on Randal Byrd."

"Hey, Frankie, let's see."

"The case came up two years ago. He was originally charged with possession of a kilo of heroin with intent to deliver. But that was thrown out when they ruled his car had been searched illegally, and he was left with a possession charge of less than a gram. His attorney — oh, you wanted his attorney's name — ah, Sam Dworkin."

"Suspenders."

"What?"

"That's what they call him: Sam 'Suspenders' Dworkin. He always wears 'em."

Francine nodded. "Well, Suspenders got him off with two years probation."

"Okay, and the judge?" Frank was moving a finger down the sheet.

"Oh, right. William J. O'Bryan was the judge."

He said nothing but produced a low hum for a few seconds.

Francine continued: "And here's something else. This guy Anthony Peoples, the one they're looking for in that car bombing? Well, you said there might be a drug connection because his cousin was some big dealer? So I looked Peoples up too. And they had him on a murder charge six months ago that was also tossed out for a lack of evidence."

"Peoples?"

"Yeah, the funny thing is he had the same attorney and the same judge. Dworkin and — what's his name — O'Bryan? They were on his case too. Isn't that weird?"

He leaned back and gazed at the ceiling for a few seconds. "Yeah, very weird. Anyway, good job. Now go call the police chief for me. Tell him we know this guy Peoples was charged with murder. And we wonder if there might be a connection with the car bombing."

Francine pointed to the paper. "Right. And here's Randal Byrd's home address and phone number."

"Francine, you're beautiful."

"Thanks, Frank!"

As Francine left, he grabbed a phone and, staring at the sheet of paper she just gave him, punched in a number.

He listened for several seconds and then spoke with a casual tone. "Hey, is this Randal Byrd?"

He listened with a furrowed frown. "Well, this is Frank DeFauw at Channel 5."

The furrows deepened. "Hello? Mr. Byrd?" Frank hung up and got to his feet while rolling down his shirt sleeves.

As he walked away he caught Dennis Clark's eye. "If I'm not back in an hour, call out the cavalry."

"Jesus, Frank, we're on in less than 90 minutes."

"Just finish the lead I was writing, and I'll be back in time."

Chapter 27

The address turned out to be less than four blocks from Marvin's Bar, a gloomy cube of a building, four stories, a three alarmer waiting to happen. He closed the Viper's door and, as he walked away, inadvertently hit the lock button on the remote twice and heard one brief blast from the horn. "Shit," he muttered as he glanced quickly away from the building. When he glanced back he found the entrance door propped wide open.

Near the back end of a dark and dirty hallway, pungent with the odor of someone's excrement, he skirted a large rat skittering in the opposite direction and minding its own business.

Stopping at what he assumed was 11A — one of the metal digits was missing, but it was right across from 10A — he knocked on the door and waited. And waited.

Finally, from inside came Byrd's voice. "Yeah?"

"Hey, Randal, it's Frank DeFauw."

After a beat Byrd sounded almost amused. "Oh, just a minute."

With a latch thrown, the door was swung half-way open. Frank found the blade of a large carving knife, swaying slightly, an inch from his nose. Randal Byrd had been drinking and, perhaps as well, indulging in something illegal. His voice was louder than it needed to be.

"Frank, for a veteran Live at 5 newsman, you're pretty fuckin' dense. I thought you'd probably get the idea I don't want to talk to you."

Frank again tried the nonchalance. "Well, Randal, I just don't like it when people hang up on me."

"I'll tell you what. You're not gone in five seconds here, I'm gonna invite you in and carve my initials on each of your fuckin' cheeks."

Frank reflexively moved a foot back from the blade. "Look, Randal, I only want to talk about what you told me at the bar about Judge O'Bryan."

"I never told you nothing about a judge. In fact, I never fuckin' seen you before in my fuckin' life. You got that, Frank? You either get the fuck outta here now, or you tell me which cheek you want me to start on."

Byrd moved forward and again brandished the blade near Frank's nose. "Better yet, maybe I start by slicin' your fuckin' nose off. How'd you look on TV without a nose, Frank?"

The sudden glint in Byrd's dead eyes made Frank back away further.

"You got the idea now? You come here again, and you leave without your fuckin' nose."

Frank nodded and continued backing away.

"Yeah, I got the idea. Have a nice day."

Chapter 28

"Randy Byrd is a shitty piece of work." In Booth Number One at the Black Knight Inn, Sam Dworkin's constantly conspiratorial rasp had been reduced almost to a whisper so his old friend Frank had to lean close to catch it.

"He's an inveterate liar—christ, his story would change every time I'd see him. He had a record as long as my arm, but small stuff mostly, bad checks, car theft, B & E, petty shit."

He stared at Dworkin. They had met a decade earlier when they served on a panel debating the merits of cameras in the courtroom, on the same side for different but equally self-serving reasons. Their friendship had grown since over their mutual love of our National Pastime, and they'd catch two or three games together each summer at Tiger Stadium.

But he realized now that he didn't really know Sam Dworkin. He had thought he liked him, knew he was smart and good at what he did, admired his encyclopedic knowledge of baseball, liked the looks of the man's pretty wife and four kids in wallet photos. But he didn't really know him.

Finally, he looked away from Dworkin and said, "But if he had some bucks stashed, say from a dope deal, it had to be tempting to milk the guy. Feed him a tale about bribing the judge when the case really went away because of a technicality."

Dworkin smiled easily. "Naw, the guy's been through the system too many times. He knows how it works. You can't pull that kind of shit on somebody like Byrd. Besides, with all the booze and drugs, his brain was fried. You don't know what he might do."

"Then why would he come up with a story like that?"

"Look, Frank, our clientele is not exactly the salt of the earth. They are scum. They will do or say anything to get what they want. Byrd, as I recall, was pissed at my fee. Here I get him off on a serious charge, and he's pissin' and moanin' about the size of the fee."

"With me he was talkin' about the judge, not you."

Exasperated, Dworkin slipped a thumb under one of his famed suspenders and snapped it.

"Frank, the guy's seen enough gossip columns to know you're pals with Billy. He's just fuckin' with your head."

Chapter 29

Turning his key in Sherie Sloan's door, he was surprised and annoyed to find the chain lock in place. "Sherie, open the door."

From inside came a new whiff of sarcasm in the woman's soft, lilting voice. "Oh, Frank, is that you? How nice." She closed the door to remove the chain, then opened it. In a long robe, she looked briefly at him, then turned and walked back into the apartment.

He followed. "Who else would have a key to an apartment I pay for?"

In the living room she sat at one end of the couch with a glass of wine on the table in front of her. "You pay for it, Frank, but I may not be here for you much longer."

He slipped off his suit coat and tossed it on a chair. "What is that supposed to mean?"

"Simple. You keep acting the way you have lately, and I'm outta here."

"The way I have lately?"

"Frank, I never see you anymore, unless it's the middle of the night. When's the last time we had dinner? But like almost every day I read about you cavorting with bimbos all over town."

He rolled up his shirt sleeves as if for fisticuffs. "'Cavorting with bimbos.' That's a catchy phrase. Sounds like you been talking with that little shit Wil Barnes."

Sherie stared at him for a second. "I told you long ago, Frank, I knew you couldn't or wouldn't leave your wife. I was okay with that. But when I don't see you, and you're running around with every cheap trick in town, it's more than I can bear."

He made a face and stretched as if his back was hurting. "You got any more wine?"

She looked at him coldly. "In the fridge."

In the kitchen he moved to the fridge but stopped when he saw magnets holding two recent Wil Barnes columns. He called back to the living room: "So you're collecting the wit and wisdom of Wil Barnes these days."

"I have to keep track of you somehow."

Opening the fridge, he removed the Chardonnay and found himself a glass. On the counter near the phone's answering machine, he spotted "Barnes" scrawled on a note pad along with a phone number. He poured himself some wine and back in the living room moved to the opposite end of the couch. "So you *have* talked with Barnes."

"What?"

He nodded toward the kitchen. "I saw his name and number. You've talked with that piece of shit, knowing damn well he wants to destroy me."

She took a sip and looked him squarely in the eye. "When I came home from work tonight the machine had a message from him."

"So you called him."

"I didn't call him."

"What did it say? The message."

"It said he wanted to talk to me about you. So obviously he knows about us."

"Obviously. If you call, we're through. You need to know that."

She held the wine in her lap, leaned back and closed her eyes. "Frank, there's almost nothing left to this relationship."

"I don't believe that. And I don't think you do either."

Those big blue eyes opened, and the woman leaned forward to speak with heat. "Believe it, Frank. I don't know if I'm gonna talk to him or not. But it would be one way to put an end to this demeaning affair once and for all."

He stared at her. "Demeaning."

"Yes, demeaning."

Chapter 30

Shortly before airtime the newsroom atmosphere was frenetic. At one end of the pit, calmly looking over a script, Frank in his shirtsleeves stood in front of a camera with a teleprompter. When a young woman with a headset pointed briskly at Frank, he looked up from the script he was holding and gazed with acute interest into the lens.

"Hello, everybody, this is Frank DeFauw. Coming up on Live News at 5: new information in that tragic car bombing two weeks ago which took the lives of a westside woman and her two children. That and more on Detroit's sky-rocketing murder rate. See you at 5."

Frank kept his gaze firmly on the camera lens until the floor director dropped her hand. Then he unclipped the mike from his tie and walked past the pit, asking, "Who's got some aspirin?"

Fingers flying over his keyboard, Dennis said, "Try Blanche."

Nearing the back of the busy newsroom, Frank called out, "Blanche, you got some aspirin?"

"I sure do. Right here in this new handy-dandy dispenser." She motioned to the corner of her desk and a gumball machine whose globe held hundreds of white tablets. "I'm gonna make me a fortune here."

Stopping in front of the desk, he reached into his pockets for some change. "What's it take?"

"Twenty dollar gold piece."

"Com'on, Blanche, the Franchise has a headache here!"

"Okay, it'll cost you a penny."

"Gonna take you a while to get rich."

He inserted a penny, pulled the lever and retrieved a tablet. As he slipped another penny in the slot, a nearby office door opened, and to Frank's mouth-dropping shock, out walked Wil Barnes, followed by News Director Jack Johanson.

A large, mustachioed man, who towered over the tiny Barnes as they shook hands, Johanson said, "Wil, thanks for coming by. Give me a call if you need anything."

"Thanks, Jack, I sure will."

A few feet away but unnoticed by these two, Frank finally found his voice: "Jesus H. Fucking Christ, Jack, I can't believe you'd actually touch this slimy hack."

Johanson turned and without great success tried to smile. "Now, Frank, behave yourself."

Frank turned to Barnes. "Who the fuck let you in this building?" And then back to Johanson: "What are we doing here, handing him a knife to carve us up?"

Johanson stopped trying to smile. "Frank, just calm down."

"You calm down, you idiot! We don't give anything to this fucking midget piece of shit."

Wil Barnes was moving for a door leading out of the newsroom. "I'll be going, folks. Thanks again."

"Get the fuck outta here before I shove you up your own asshole."

Smiling as he headed out the door, Barnes said, "See ya, Frank. Give my best to Sherie."

Frank started after him. "You little cunt..."

Johanson grabbed Frank in a bear hug before he could move more than a step. "Hold on, Frank. He's not worth it."

Frank screamed, "Leave her alone, Barnes, or I swear to God, I'll cut off your fuckin' balls."

Everybody in the newsroom was up watching, some actually standing on chairs to get a better view, as Johanson continued to hug his franchise.

Chapter 31

In well-worn boxers the black man was again sitting on his bare mattress and watching Frank on his ancient, small-screened TV. He was listening intently to the anchor's well-modulated delivery.

"Police still refuse to say if Anthony Peoples is a suspect in the car bombing two weeks ago which took the lives of his wife and two children. But Channel 5 has learned that six months ago Peoples was charged with first degree murder in the shooting death of a security guard during the armed robbery of a party store on the Detroit's westside."

When a mug shot photo of Anthony Peoples appeared full-screen, the man fingered a small video cassette next to him on the mattress.

"The charge against Peoples was later dropped because of what the Wayne County Prosecutor's office called a lack of sufficient evidence. But police are investigating Peoples' apparent underworld connections. His cousin, Richard 'Pretty Rick' Mahone, was reputed to be one of this area's major narcotics importers. Mahone, who was said to prefer one of his other nicknames, 'Maserati Rick,' was murdered two months ago in what police described as a mob-style execution. Police have been looking for Peoples ever since a bomb planted in his car outside his westside home killed his wife and two children. Peoples was not believed to have been at home when the blast occurred. But he hasn't been seen since, and police understandably have a few questions for him."

Frank's delivery upped its intensity. "We at Channel 5 have offered to help Mr. Peoples safely reach the law enforcement agency of his choice and to tell his side of the story. Again, Mr. Peoples, if you're watching..."

In the hot, grubby little room the mattress was now empty. Frank was still speaking from the screen in fluttery black and white.

"...please give me a call here at the station, and I will personally meet with you at the time and place of your choosing."

Chapter 32

On opposite corners of this bombed-out city intersection were a dirty, littered, sad excuse for a park and a crumbling, abandoned apartment building with the glass smashed in nearly every window of its four floors.

Two groups of black males occuppied the corners: one in their 40s and 50s in the park, lounging on broken benches or perched on crates, passing something in small paper bags; the other in their mid-teens in front of the apartment hulk, serving the drive-up trade at curbside.

On a third corner the man who had been watching Frank so closely, now in wrap-around sunglasses, jeans and a Hank Aaron "755" t-shirt, walked to a phone booth, reached in and lifted the receiver.

Chapter 33

In the WTEM control room, the newscast continued. On the line monitor Mary Scott was saying, "...and in just a moment Don Allard talks to the mother of that 14-month-old girl who was killed by a stray bullet that crashed through her living room window last month."

With a small flourish of his left hand the director said, "And black."

At a console next to the director, Dennis Clark pushed a button and leaned toward a mike. "Good work guys, right on the money." In front of Dennis a phone buzzed, and he picked it up. "Control Room." Dennis paused and shook his head. "Ah, sir, he's on the air right now in the middle of a newscast."

In the studio during the break Frank and Mary were shuffling through their scripts. Frank said, "Hey, Mare, you ever tried this Ice stuff, smokeable speed? I hear it's great for PMS."

"Shove it, Frank."

Dennis's amplified voice filled the studio. "Frank, a guy on the phone says he's Anthony Peoples."

Dropping his script, Frank said, "Put him through."

Dennis: "You've got less than forty seconds."

The phone buzzed under the desk, and Frank picked it up. "Hi, this is Frank DeFauw." He paused, pulled a pen from his suit coat, turned his script over and wrote on the back. "Okay, I'll be there by 7:30."

Chapter 34

On the street corner the man in the sunglasses still held the receiver.

"One other thing, man. I'll know if you're bein' followed. So make sure you're not. Or the trip'll be for nothin'."

When he hung up, his eye caught something scribbled with a black marker on the plastic window of the booth next to the phone.

detroit im dyin

only come here on a dare

detroit im dyin

dont you even fuckin care

He had seen this someplace else. Spray-painted on the wall of a school off Cass Avenue. So some wanna-be poet was loose on these desperate streets, or maybe others were copying it here and there.

Whatever, the words were lodged with an ache at the base of his stomach.

Moving out of the booth, he swept his gaze from the enterprising youngsters on one corner to the broken down bench brigade on the other.

Then he walked away, wondering how long he could keep hiding in plain site in this god-forsaken city.

Chapter 35

With maybe two hours of daylight left, the sun low and in his eyes, he slipped on his shades and drove the Viper quickly through light traffic. Checking the rear-view mirror he noted a black Taurus a block and a half back. He made two right turns. The Taurus was still back there.

Thirteen minutes later the Viper pulled up at the covered side entrance to the Westin Hotel in the huge multi-building Renaissance Center complex on the river. As he slid out of the car, a valet guy was on him quickly.

"Frank, how are you this evening?"

"Hey, good. I'll be awhile."

"Very good, sir."

Heading for the entrance, he glanced about 40 yards up the street and found the Taurus stopped at the curb.

Once inside he kept the shades in place and walked with pace through the lobby past a huge floral arrangement on a marble-topped table. As usual it was quiet in this cavernous place, and drawing none of the usual greetings and stares, he turned down a circular corridor lined with a few shops and eating places and, moving quickly now, headed for another, larger lobby off an entrance on another side of the complex.

When he emerged from the riverside entrance, he promptly flagged a passing cab. Sitting low in the backseat, he slipped a furtive look at the empty entrance as the taxi pulled away, and the cabbie asked where to.

Chapter 36

The sun was still up in the west over the city. From this roof-top corner of a three-story building, there was a clear view of both streets converging to form an intersection below. Little or no traffic moved in this mostly abandoned industrial area. Finally a taxi was headed this way, moving up one of the streets that fronted this building. A car followed the cab but then turned off on a cross street.

From inside the cab Frank took a close look at what used to be a small factory. From the rotting plywood covering the windows and the crumbling masonry, it appeared nothing had been produced here in many years. The cabbie stopped in front and said, "You sure you got the right address?"

Frank got out. "Just keep it running, buddy, and wait here."

From the rooftop corner, the black man in the wrap-arounds watched Frank stand next to the cab, glance up and down the empty street and move to the entrance.

To Frank's surprise the battered old door opened easily. The hallway inside was dark and decrepit and filled with a stench so bad he could hardly breathe. Maybe dead animals, he thought. Moving cautiously through, he found a stairwell and headed up. A grimey window on a landing above provided just enough light for him to see the dirty, littered steps. As he climbed he began to feel it in his knees and resolved to get back to the Stairmaster.

At the top of the last flight, he pushed on a door, and it creaked open only with considerable effort. Stepping out into the light on a flat, tarred roof full of cracks and holes, he found no one in sight.

Then from behind the door, a black man appeared and removed his wrap-arounds.

"Didn't think you'd come."

Frank turned to face him, and the two stared at each other.

"You don't look much like your mug shot, but Mr. Peoples, I presume."

"I'm not lookin' like my driver's license neither." He held his license next to his face. "But yeah, that's me."

Frank looked closely first at the license and then at the face, now covered with a heavy beard and framed with budding dreadlocks. "Okay, yeah, so you're Anthony."

"Were you followed?"

"Yeah, but I lost 'em. Why would I be followed?"

"You don't know these people."

"What people?"

"People blew up my family."

Frank shook his head. "I can't imagine how you're dealing with that, Anthony. So who did it and why?"

Anthony Peoples gazed hard at Frank before answering. "Look, you gotta understand some things first."

"I'm all ears."

"The first thing is I had nothin' to do with that robbery at the party store and shootin' that security guard."

"Right."

"No, this is for real, man. I'm in there that night to buy some beer, and this guy that did the deal walks in. There's just this one Arab girl behind the counter, and she knew me from the neighborhood. The guy pulls a gun, she gets all scared and confused. And when the shootin' started with the guard, I hit the floor, then split and just run home. She tells the cops I was with the guy. And the guy, tryin' to get hisself a plea deal, says, yeah, I was the look out."

"But you're saying you had nothing to do with it at all."

"Swear to God, man."

"Okay. So what's this about your cousin being 'Pretty Rick'?"

"Rick was my cousin. I grew up with him. But the last five, six years I had nothin' to do with him. Still, when I got charged, he went the bail and hired me his attorney. Big time guy named Dworkin."

"Sam."

"Yeah, so he says he can get my case to this judge, and he'll toss it if I give him fifty grand."

"Judge Billy O'Bryan?"

"How'd you know?"

"I looked it up. But, hold on, you had fifty grand?"

"No, man, not even close."

"So why the hell would they think you could come up with it?"

74

The black man shrugged. "Probably figured I could get it easy from Rick."

Frank shook his head. "I have to tell you, Anthony, this is not making a hell of lot of sense."

"It's the truth, man."

"Okay, so what happened next?"

"So next I went to Gant."

Frank was incredulous. "Prentis Gant, the prosecutor?"

"Yeah, my wife Nita said, 'You are nothin' but innocent. You go to the prosecutor and tell him about this. And so I did."

"And Gant said what?"

"And Gant says he's been tryin' to get something on these guys for a long time. So we end up gettin' it all on video tape with Dworkin and the judge."

"Wait, wait, so you got a pay-off with these guys on tape?"

"Yeah, but before Gant could do anything, they found out about it. Must be somebody in his office. And they squeezed Gant to drop it."

"Squeezed how?"

"I don't know, but Gant's wife is Mexican. Half her family's here, maybe illegally."

Frank nodded and stared off for a few seconds before saying, "Okay, so what about the bomb?"

"So Gant called me before it happened. He said it'd be good to get my family out of town. Said I had to meet with him that night and to bring the tape."

"You had the tape?"

"Copy of it, yeah. That was the deal I had with Gant. I thought havin' a copy of the tape would be protection. But I was gettin' that tape when the car blew up. Nita, she didn't know nothin' about this. Gant said I couldn't tell nobody about it, even my wife, so I didn't want her seein' me get the tape. So I said take the kids out and start the car."

"So then you *were* at the house when it happened. The police have been saying you weren't."

"No, they don't know. I was there, in the basement. I didn't see it happen, but I heard it." He paused for a moment. "And by the time I go upstairs and look, it was so far bad, I knew they were all of them gone." He stopped and stared at the sun heading down.

Frank said nothing.

"Jesus, I didn't know what to do, so I just split, down the alley and out of the hood, and nobody even seen me with all the cops and ambulances coming and the sirens goin'."

He looked back at Frank. "But I mean, Nita and the babies, they wasn't even supposed to be in town. Supposed to be in Chicago, but our van had to go in the shop."

Frank shook his head again and finally asked, "So you still have the tape?"

"Not with me, no, but, yeah, I got it."

"Why did you call me, Anthony?"

"'Cause I don't trust any cops, even the feds, 'til this whole thing is public."

"So why trust me?"

"I don't really know, man. I really don't. Specially when I read about you and the judge being' pals in the newspaper."

"You're reading a guy that hates me. And besides, if the judge is dirty, no friendship's gonna save him."

"Yeah, well, anyway, there's no one else left for me. And I'm not figurin' to just disappear. They're gonna pay for what they done."

Frank looked at him for a long time, studying the saddest eyes he'd ever seen. Finally, he put out his hand, and Anthony shook it. And then Frank surprised himself, grabbing the man and giving him a hug.

When he looked into those eyes again, he said, "I'll have to do some checking, Anthony. But the next time I see you, I'll need that tape."

Peoples nodded. "My life, man, what's left of it, it's in your hands."

Chapter 37

At 9:30 it was quiet in the night-side newsroom. Francine was working at one computer and reporter Don Allard at another. Frank walked in with energy and purpose.

"Francine, can you get me Prentis Gant's home address."

"Right away, Frank."

Frank moved past Allard. "How you doing, Don?"

"Good, Frank. You see Barnes' column?"

"Tonight?"

"Yeah, another blind item. I don't know how he gets away with that shit. If we did anything like that, they'd run us out of town."

Frank scooped up a copy of the Freep as he walked past a desk. "You got that right."

Francine remembered something and turned away from her computer. "Frank, Alice left word. She wants to see you. I think Jack's with her."

He stopped abruptly. "At this hour?"

"Yes, she said as soon as you came in."

Chapter 38

Reading the paper folded over, Frank was walking down a long hallway. He stopped, finished what he was reading, then shook his head in disgust and walked again.

In the VP-GM's suite the secretary's desk was buttoned up. Frank entered and moved through to stand in the doorway to Alice Whitney's office. Alice was at her desk, and with his pipe clamped in his mouth, Jack Johanson occupied a chair. Between them on the desk was the same paper Frank had been reading.

He walked in. "So, burning the midnight oil."

Alice looked up. "How are you, Frank?"

"I'm fine, Alice, and you?" He moved to another chair in front of the desk, ignoring Johanson. "Why so late?"

"I was catching up. These quarterly reports always put me behind. And Jack and I were talking about Barnes."

Frank nodded. "Ah, Jack's favorite journalist."

The news director looked at the ceiling and said, "You're my favorite journalist, Frank."

Frank promptly dropped his cool. "Oh, horseshit, Jack. I can't remember the last time you gave a newspaper guy an interview. You must think Barnes is something so special that you..."

Alice intervened. "Frank, I asked Jack to see Barnes."

Frank's head shook with disgust. "When are you guys ever gonna learn he's a snake? He'll take all your schmoozing and then turn around and bite you in the ass. Or rather, bite me in the ass. He's a fuckin' snake."

Alice stared him firmly in the eye. "He may be a snake, Frank, but he writes this town's most widely read column every other day. He can bite you in the ass whenever he feels like it. What's the old line, 'Never get, into a pissing match with an elephant?'"

"With a skunk" laughed Frank. "'Never get into a pissing match with a skunk.' I love it when you gals try to be one of the boys."

Alice bowed her head briefly with annoyance. "Look, Frank, Jack and I've been talking, and we think it might be a good idea if you took some time off."

"What?" For the second time this night Frank was shocked.

Alice knew she'd finally got his attention. "You seem to be under a lot of pressure lately, Frank. And the fact is you've been through a lot in the past year. Take some time off. Get things patched up at home. Stay out of the spotlight for a while and get your life together."

He stared at her dumbfounded as Alice sailed on. "The fact is you seem to be drinking more than you should again. And lately it seems to be affecting your work. You're not as sharp. And frankly, your judgment seems to be lacking, especially in public situations that are bound to find their way into print with Wil Barnes in this town."

He felt himself getting mobilized. "I can't believe this. Is this all because of a stupid little three-line item in Barnes' column tonight?" Picking up the folded-over newspaper he'd been holding, he read:

"'Which local media prince is battling booze and the blues with both his wife and his long-time mistress? Friends say both women have had it with him and want a divorce.'"

He looked up at Alice. "Christ, most people won't even know who he's talking about."

She shook her head. "Give your audience more credit than that, Frank."

Johanson said, "Look, Frank, Barnes says there's a lot more where that came from. He says he has a date with Sherie to spill her guts about you and booze and drugs and other women."

For the first time Frank felt a stab of something close to fear. "Barnes is a fucking liar!"

"I'm sure he is," said Johanson. "But apparently he's working on a major spread that names names and could appear as early as Sunday. That's what I was doing with him today, Frank—damage control, giving him quote after quote about what a remarkable journalist you are. All of which I believe, by the way."

Alice tried a woman's touch. "Look, Frank, we're on your side. All we're concerned about is you and your family. And we really think you should take some time off."

Staring down at the paper in his lap, Frank seemed beaten. But when he looked up, there was a powerful appeal in his eyes. "Alice,

I'm working on what could be the biggest expose we've ever done here. Bigger than that thing with the mayor's family a few years ago. And the one thing I need right now is air time. Don't take me off."

She glanced at Johanson, who looked more than a little dubious. "What's the story, Frank?"

"I can't tell you right now. It involves some powerful guys in this town who happen to be friends of mine. And I don't want to say anything until I've absolutely nailed it down. Look, you wanted me to take some time off? Take me off tonight's eleven and maybe tomorrow's. Don's in the newsroom. He can sit in for me. I could really use the time to work on this story."

Johanson was rolling his eyes and shaking his head as Alice glanced at him again. He said, "No, this is crazy. You've got to tell us something."

"Look, it's that car bombing we had last month. Tonight I met with the guy whose family was blown away. And the next time I see him, I may have the whole thing wrapped up with a bow."

Alice stared at Johanson who puffed on his pipe.

Chapter 39

In the darkness enveloping this carefully-manicured, upper-middle-class residential street, Frank stepped out of the Viper. He had parked under one of the three dead streetlights on this block, and pausing to check out the large, nicely-kept older home in front of him, he made a note to tell the desk there was a story here: even in Sherwood Forrest, one of its few well-to-do and well-connected neighborhoods, this hapless city couldn't keep the streetlights on.

As he walked toward the home, his quick scan of the block missed a car parked a hundred yards behind the Viper. In it a man in a black hooded sweatshirt over a black baseball cap sat low behind the wheel and watched Frank proceed up the front walk.

On the porch Frank rang the bell, and after a short wait, the inside door opened, and the former county prosecutor Prentis Gant appeared at the screen door.

"Hi, Frank DeFauw, Mr. Gant. We've talked in the past."

After an awkward pause: "Right. What can I do for you?"

"If you've got a few minutes, I'd like to come in and talk with you."

Gant looked exhausted and uttered an audible sigh. "Frank, it's 11 o'clock at night, and I've retired from public life."

"I know that, but I spoke with Anthony Peoples tonight, and he said some things I'd like to check with you."

Gant looked past Frank toward the street, then unlocked and opened the screen. "Well, I can give you a few minutes, but I'm sure there's nothing I can help you with."

The man watching from the car down the block saw Frank step into the house. Moving out of the car, the man walked up the street.

Inside the home, as he usherd Frank through a spotless, well-appointed living room, Gant said, "Let's sit on the back porch."

"Fine."

As they moved past a staircase, an Hispanic woman was standing half-way down in a long dressing gown.

The woman spoke softly with an accent: "What is it, Prent?"

Gant stopped and looked up. "Ah, Dee, this is Frank DeFauw from TV. Frank, my wife Delores."

With a deeply concerned look, she nodded as Frank said, "Hi, Delores. Sorry to bother you at this hour."

"No bother." she said, keeping her gaze on her husband.

Gant said, "Honey, we'll only be a few minutes. Are the kids asleep?"

"I think so."

"Why don't you check on them, and I'll be up shortly."

Delores tried a smile. "Sure." She nodded again at Frank, turned and moved back up the stairs. The two men continued toward the back of the house and moved on to a large screened-in porch. Gant motioned him to a rattan chair and said, "You spoke with Peoples."

As he answered, "Yes, I did," a cat yowled outside the porch and pawed at the screen. Gant unlocked and opened the door, saying, "C'mon, Sailor." The black and white shorthair took a nervous look at Frank and moved quickly through the porch and into the house.

Frank decided he'd better get right to the point. "Yeah, so he told me he worked with you to get evidence for a bribery case against Judge O'Bryan and Sam Dworkin."

Sitting in another rattan piece across from Frank, Gant shifted and stared at him for a few seconds. Finally, he said, "All I can tell you about Peoples is what you probably already know. Some months ago he was charged with armed robbery and felony murder. And the charges were later dropped because of a lack of evidence."

Frank nodded. "He said because of the bribery case, you were forced to resign and his family was murdered in the car bombing."

Gant shook his head and spoke quickly. "I resigned for the reasons I stated at the time. Obviously I know nothing about the car bombing."

"Peoples told me he has a videotape of the payoff."

Again without hesitation: "I have no knowledge of what Peoples has."

"He said your wife has relatives here in the states illegally, and that's what they used to pressure you."

"My wife has no relatives here."

He stared hard at Gant. "That's all you're gonna say?"

"That's all there is to say." Gant was already on his feet. "I'm sorry I can't help you any further."

Chapter 40

Outside the Gant home, the man in the black cap and sweatshirt was moving along one side of the yard toward the screened-in back porch. As he peered around a large, thick bush and into the porch, he saw the two men walking back into the house.

Waiting several seconds, he then moved to the screen door and tried the handle.

Silently Gant led Frank past the stairway, back through the living room into the front vestibule. He opened the heavy oak door and pushed the screen open. In close quarters he turned and spoke firmly a few inches from Frank's face. "I don't know what you think you're doing with Peoples's story, Frank, but I would strongly advise you to let law enforcement handle it. You're playing a dangerous game at the moment, and you're likely to get somebody hurt."

Frank moved past Gant and out the door. "Thanks for the advice, Mr. Gant. You change your mind, just give me a call."

Gant said nothing, and Frank moved down the front walk.

Chapter 41

Parting the curtains at a second-floor bedroom window, Delores Gant looked outside. She watched Frank as he walked to his little roadster and got in. Once the car began to drive away, the woman moved back to a four-year-old boy sitting up in bed. She gave him a warm hug and kiss.

Then a sharp crack came from somewhere below in the house. The woman froze with a stricken look, then laid the child down and said "Mamma will be right back."

Leaving the room, she grabbed the railing in the hall at the top of the stairs and called, "Prent?"

Descending the stairs, she stopped again near the bottom. "Prent!"

Now she moved down the last two steps and walked cautiously through a dining room to the double doors that led to the screened-in porch. "Darling, where are you?"

When she reached the doorway and looked in she uttered a forlorn wail. Her husband was sprawled face down on the porch floor. A pool of blood was already forming from a wound in his temple. A pistol she had never seen before was nestled in his right hand.

Chapter 42

The morning sun was still low in the east, glinting in his eyes as he stood at a front window watching the two men get into a black Chevy sedan parked on the circular drive in front of the house.

"Mutt and Jeff," he muttered and went looking for Marci.

He found her looking remarkably good in a white dressing gown that showed off her tan, her sun-streaked hair up in a way he had always found fetching, sitting with a mug of coffee at the glass-top table on the deck and gazing at the lake.

In his slacks and golf shirt, he stepped from the house onto the deck, and she turned to him and asked softly, "What did they want?"

He sat at the table. "The cops? They wanted to talk to me about the ex-prosecutor Prentis Gant."

"Why you?"

"He was found dead last night, and they think I was the last person to see him alive."

"My god, Frank. What happened?"

He was staring off but turned his gaze back to her. She still had the lightest hazel eyes he'd ever seen, and they always seemed even lighter when she was surprised. "After I left his home about 11 o'clock last night, they say he put a gun to his head and blew his brains out."

"Jesus, Mary, Joseph."

"So they wanted to know what we talked about and whether he seemed suicidal."

"What did you tell them?"

"Not much. I said what we talked about was strictly business and confidential. And that he did not seem depressed."

There were times, he knew, when Marci clearly did not want to know what her husband knew, but this was not one of them. "What do you think happened?"

"I think he may have been murdered."

"Murdered?"

He said nothing and again turned his gaze away.

"Why? By whom?"

He still said nothing, but he knew this would not work with his wife.

"Frank!"

Still not looking at her Frank said, "Perhaps by our friend Judge Billy."

When he turned back to her, she looked as if she had failed to comprehend his words. "Frank, that's...crazy. How could you even think Billy would be capable of murder?"

He gave her a dead-on look and said, "Hey, you said a while back that he was perfectly capable of taking a bribe. And Prentis Gant may have had proof that Billy was doing just that."

When her look showed that she had begun to comprehend, he added, "That's what we were talking about last night."

"So what did he say?"

"Gant? He wouldn't say anything. But there may have been three other murders connected to this as well. Remember that car bombing last month?"

"Of course I remember."

"Well..."

"Frank, taking a bribe is one thing, but murder? I don't believe for a minute that Billy could do anything like that."

He got up and walked away from the table toward the house. "Well, I'll offer your vote of confidence the next time I see him."

As he was about to step through the door to the kitchen, she stopped him. "Frank, I need to tell you something."

Not liking the tone or the feel of this, he turned and stared at his wife. "What is it?"

"I've asked my attorney to file."

Suddenly short of breath, as if slugged in the gut, he continued to stare. Finally, he said, "Marci, please don't do this right now."

"I'm sorry, Frank. I just can't take it anymore. I hope we can do this in a way that's fair and friendly. That's certainly my intention."

He nodded and looked at the lake. "Right, fair and friendly." His breathing still felt labored, and he tried to keep it silent. Don't show her what you're feeling, he thought. But then, he wondered, what the hell *was* he feeling?

Was this actually the golden chance he'd been waiting for to grab a new life with Sherie? But then what did "Please don't do this right now" mean? Was it just that the moment was inconvenient? That there were too many distractions in his life right now to give their marriage a serious look? Was he just too damn busy? Of course, that was nonsense, and he was being a bloody fool.

He suddenly felt flushed with a desperate, hopeless ache and felt a powerful urge to go to her right now, get on his knees and, ready to make any damn promise she might extract, beg her forgiveness. But when he finally glanced her way, she had turned her back to him. As if to say, "I don't give a jot what you're feeling or thinking. It's over and done."

Chapter 43

In the news studio at Channel 5, a large, computer-generated globe spun on a screen behind the news desk where Frank and Mary waited for the stage manager's pointed finger. When it came, he began:

"In news from around the nation and around the world: Today in Washington, day one of the first official Russian-American summit, President George Bush and Russian president Boris Yeltsin met and agreed in principle to major reductions in nuclear weapons."

In the hallway outside the studio, on a cabinet that also held a coffee urn, a TV set showed Bush and Yeltsin smiling broadly and shaking hands as Frank's voice-over continued: "Yeltsin consented to an end of the concept of parity in the number of strategic arms..."

Normally there for the stagehands waiting for those studio doors to open, the coffee and TV were now being used by two strangers, one tall, white and heavyset, the other short, black and trim. Both dressed in suits and ties, the big guy was rumpled, the small one a bit of a dandy.

"Bush and Yeltsin agreed that by 2003 the U.S. would have 3500 warheads and the Russians 3000. At present both countries have about 10,000 warheads. Mary?"

On the TV a 2-shot turned into a close up of Mary's frigid smile. "Frank, also today, Caspar Weinberger, who served as Secretary of Defense under President Ronald Reagan, was indicted in the Iran Contra case..."

In her office, Alice Whitney kept her eyes on the center set of her three built-into-the-wall TVs but told news director, "We all know he can be a pain, but you need to talk to her about the vitriol. It's just becoming way too apparent."

Johanson puffed on his pipe. "I'll talk to both of them."

Mary continued: "...Prosecutors investigating the arms scandal charged that Weinberger had committed perjury in Congressional testimony and that he had obstructed justice. Weinberger claims he refused to plead guilty to a lesser offense and called his indictment a 'moral and legal outrage.'"

The two strangers were still watching the set outside the studio as Frank said: "And finally, last week, you'll remember, Vice-President Dan Quayle stood up for traditional family values. Well, yesterday Mr. Quayle advised a contestant at this spelling bee in Trenton, New Jersey, to add an 'e' to the spelling of 'potato.'"

As the dandy looked at his watch, Frank added: "Perhaps, Mr. Vice-President, you might consider getting yourself some traditional education."

Chapter 44

As the studio doors swung open Mary stalked out first and smiled reflexively at the two strangers waiting a few feet away. Walking out behind her, Frank spotted them quickly.

"Well, if it ain't Mutt and Jeff. Hey, fellas, how's the detective business?"

The dandy smirked. "Busy, Frank, but we need to do a little follow up on some of the things you told us yesterday. Would you have a few minutes for us?"

"Sure, no problem. How about my office."

As they walked, no one spoke, and Frank tried to remember their names. The big one in the same wrinkled black suit as yesterday was Hal something. The small black guy, spotless in beige with a gold stick pin and cufflinks, had a strange first one. Fontaine.

In his office he grabbed a stack of files off the couch and piled them on his cluttered desk. The two detectives used the couch. He sat behind his desk and asked, "So what can I do for you, guys? It's Hal and Fontaine, right?"

Fontaine had done most of the talking yesterday, and it started that way again. "Right. You've got a good memory."

"No, I've got a great memory. Cursed with it, really."

"So, Frank, we wanted to follow up on a couple things you talked about yesterday."

As Frank was nodding, the big guy finally opened his mouth: "And a couple a things you wouldn't talk about."

Fontaine shot a quick glance at his partner. "Yeah, that too. Now first of all, a couple of little things. You said you had met Mrs. Gant on the stairway, and she went back upstairs, presumably to take care of their children. Did you ever see or hear anything from her other than that one time?"

"No, I told you that yesterday."

"Right. Did you hear any sounds in the house, upstairs or down, while you were there talking to Gant?"

"Sounds?"

"Yeah, like floors creaking, doors opening or closing, anything at all?"

He thought for a few seconds. "No, I don't think so. But I was just concentrating on what he was saying."

"And what about when the cat came into the house?"

"The cat?"

"Yes, what about when Gant let the cat in the porch door. You said the front door was locked while you were there, because when you left, Gant unlocked the front door to let you out."

"Right, that's what I said."

Fontaine leaned forward a bit on the couch. "So when Gant let the cat in the screened porch at the back of the house, did he unlock the door?"

"Well, I told you yesterday I thought he did, but he opened it quickly and I was a little distracted by what we were talking about, so I couldn't be sure. And to anticipate your next question, no, I simply can't remember seeing him lock it after the cat came in. He may have, and I may have seen it, but right now I have no image of that in my head. Sorry. I mean, I remember he called the cat 'Sailor,' and it was a smallish black and white with short hair. Maybe I was paying too much attention to the cat to notice what he did with the lock."

Fontaine nodded his little head. "Okay. Now you told us yesterday that Mr. Gant did not appear depressed to you. On what exactly did you base that assessment?"

"That assessment. Well, I guess, because, while he was subdued, he was not, as the shrinks like to say, without affect. He seemed warm and affectionate in the brief exchange with his wife. He was direct and focused in his comments to me. He wasn't vague or foggy. He just didn't seem depressed. As I told you, I wasn't there that long, maybe not even 10 minutes. I guess the one who could really tell you about him is his wife."

Fontaine raised his chin in a half-nod, then sat back on the couch. As if on cue, Hal spoke from his slouch. "So you say you were a little distracted by what you and Gant were talking about. Tell us again what that was."

Frank got up from the desk to move around his messy office. "I can't tell you again, because I never told you in the first place. As I said yesterday, we were talking business, and I consider it confidential."

Hal didn't move as he watched Frank sit on the edge of the desk and loom over them. "You consider it confidential. Why would that be, since the guy is dead?"

"Doesn't matter. It's the principle of the thing. We were talking off the record, and confidentiality is still important whether the person is alive or not."

Hal stirred his big body until it was more upright on the couch. "Look, DeFauw, we're just tryin' to do our job. This guy was a prominent member of the community. He may have killed hisself, or maybe he was murdered. What you were talking to him about could very well help figure this thing out. Seems like you could tell us at least in general terms what you went there to talk to him about."

"Okay, in general terms, I was just doing my job. I was asking him about why he resigned. Here he is a relatively young guy, and after only a year on the job, he resigns. Why?"

"So what'd he say?"

"Nope, that's all I can say. Besides, he really didn't tell me anything he hadn't already said in public. There, now you got the whole damn thing."

"And that's all you asked about, why he resigned."

"Right."

"So you go to his house at 11 o'clock at night to ask him why he resigned. The fuck is that about?"

"It's about doing my job. I was off the 11 that night, so I thought I'd make use of the time. You guys know something about long hours, don't you? Same thing."

Hal glanced at Fontaine, and the two got to their feet. Looking testy, the big guy said, "No, it ain't the same thing, Frank. We're trying to get at the truth here, and you're tryin' to cover it up."

Frank just looked at them and shook his head.

Fontaine started for the door, then stopped. "One last thing. Why were you off the 11?"

"No special reason. I had lots of work to do, checking out stories like Gant's resignation. Besides, we were out of the book, the major ratings period, so they gave me the night off."

Hal and Fontaine looked at each other and nodded together.

Chapter 45

The next afternoon in his office he asked Fay to have dinner with him later, and as usual she said no. "There's just too much going on with this Gant thing."

"You're such a conscientious little producer."

"Hey, speaking of which, you saw where Barnes attached that word to you, right?"

"Surely you joke."

"You didn't read Barnes today?"

"I don't read that prick anymore. Not good for my health. But if you're saying he called me that, we need to have your eyes checked."

"I think it was 'devoted and conscientious.' You need to hear this." She took a piece from the Freep off her clipboard.

"Devoted and conscientious about what? Booze and broads?"

"Here, just listen." She read from the column:

"'Police investigating the mysterious death of former Wayne County prosecutor Prentice Gant are miffed at Channel 5's legendary anchor boy Frank 'Frankie Franchise' DeFauw.

"'As reported elsewhere in this edition, police now think DeFauw may have been the last person to see Gant alive Tuesday night shortly before the former prosecutor was shot to death in his own home.

"'Investigators trying to determine whether the death was a suicide or a homicide feel DeFauw could be "a lot more forthcoming and helpful" in their investigation.

"'What's puzzling to this Ink Stained Wretch is why such a devoted and conscientious newsman as Defauw has failed in his own reporting to mention anything about his own role in the story of Gant's tragic passing.

"'So what gives, Frankie? Why so silent about a major facet of what might be the biggest story you'll report on this year?'"

When she looked up from the paper, he said slowly, "Un-fucking-believable."

"You'll need to say something tonight, right?"

"Yeah, I'll say something. But, look, I knew those cops were pissed I wouldn't talk because of confidentiality, but to feed that asshole shit like this is really too much."

"Maybe he made that up."

"About the cops saying I wasn't forthcoming? Yeah, he's fully capable."

"So I'll call the copshop and get a statement from them. And you know what they'll say."

"Yeah, 'We never comment to the press on an on-going investigation.'"

"That'll be good to use. It'll call into question Barnes' whole column. But, Frank, let me ask you something."

"What?"

"Why have you kept me out of this whole thing? You've been so secret about all this stuff with Gant and Anthony Peoples. And now I think Judge O'Bryan is part of it too. I mean, you've been asking little Francine, who's brand new, to make calls for you. Why don't you trust me?"

With a sidelong glance, he said, "Hey, Fay, a tad jealous here?"

"Frank, please, you know me better than that. I'm just puzzled."

"Look, I haven't even told Alice or Jack much about it. And I'll never tell anybody unless it really pans out. I should know in the next day or so, and if it does, I'll need your help big time. Oh, and the reason I asked Francine to make calls is precisely *because* she's brand new. If I had asked you, you'd have the whole thing figured out by now."

She gave him a mock smile. "Frank, you are such a bull-shitter."

Chapter 46

Alice Whitney was alone in her large office, her desk buried in paperwork that needed her attention before she could go home this evening. Glancing up at her large monitors, she noted Frank ready to start his commentary, snatched the remote and pumped the volume.

"Tonight I need to say a few words about the death of former Wayne County prosecutor Prentice Gant and about some false and irresponsible charges a self-described Ink Stained Wretch has made in today's Detroit Free Press."

Alice shook her head. She knew exactly why she put up with the man's pain-in-the-ass antics. Without him, the station would be looking, not at a two-point lead, but at third place in the latest book. Still, and in spite of his argument that to pull him now would look like they were caving in this latest little dust up with Barnes, she had been sorely tempted to put him on the shelf for awhile. When he admitted he had not heard again from Anthony Peoples and that his big expose was on hold, she had said it was probably time for that respite she had mentioned the other day. He had actually started getting red in the face.

"Christ, Alice! The one thing I need now is airtime. Everything depends on it. The fact is I'm three weeks away from taking a week with the family down at our home on the island."

Would she regret not standing firm? Quite possibly.

On the monitor Frank continued: "Gant was a talented young prosecutor, apparently on the criminal justice fast track until three weeks ago when he resigned to, as he put it at the time, spend more time with his family and 'pursue other interests.' Then two nights ago Mr. Gant was found dead in his home with a gunshot wound to the head.

"It is true, as reported in the Free Press, that I had spoken with Mr. Gant in his home earlier in the evening. But in the gossipy drivel Wil Barnes palms off as a column today, he makes the absurd claim that I have not cooperated fully with police investigators in the case. According to Barnes, police told him that I could be—quote—'a lot more forthcoming and helpful'—unquote. This is completely false and libelous."

Chapter 47

In his big, comfortable, high-ceilinged family room, holding golden-haired, four-year-old Missy in his lap, William O'Bryan looked between the Seuss book he was reading to her and the TV where his old school chum was saying things the judge wanted to hear.

"Today I called the police detectives who interviewed me to ask if they or anyone in the department had complained about me to Mr. Barnes. The answer I got was this, and I quote: 'Frank, as you well know, our strict policy is to never talk to any member of the press or the media about details of an on-going investigation.'"

Gazing at her RCA and running a tanned and freckled hand through her cascade of red curls, Letty Pell was spending more effort on gauging the lines on his face than on the substance of what he was saying.

"So, folks, here are the facts: I have answered every question from police investigators as fully as possible. I have given them every bit of information I have that could relate in any way to what happened to Mr. Gant. And I have not injected myself in any of the reporting we've done on the tragic death of Prentice Gant, for the simple reason that I played no role in this story whatsoever. I met with Mr. Gant in my capacity as a newsman to ask if he would elaborate on why he had cut short such a promising career. We talked only for a few minutes and broke no new ground."

Anthony Peoples sat up straight on his bare mattress, his eyes locked on the old TV portable as Frank continued.

"I suppose I could have sensationalized my accidental proximity to this sad event in our news shows over the past two days. But that would have been irresponsible, and it's not how we do things here at Channel 5.

"Finally, I want to take a moment to offer the condolences of everyone here at Channel 5 to Mr. Gant's widow, Delores and their two children, Samuel, aged 4 and Rebecca, aged 2."

On his feet now, the black man glanced briefly around his squalid excuse for a room, then, with one quick look back at Frank shuffling papers at the anchor desk, grabbed his soiled old backpack and left.

Chapter 48

With the phone ringing as he walked into his mess of an office, he lifted the receiver. "DeFauw."

Gladys, who handled calls after 6 at the back desk, said, "Frank, I got a man on the line says his name is Peoples?"

"Great, Glad, put him on." He stretched the phone cord and reached for the office door to swing it shut.

"Hullo." The voice sounded sullen.

"Anthony, is that you?"

"Yeah, it's me."

"Great, so how you doin', man. I've been worried about you."

"Yeah, well, I'm not doin' so good."

"What's up Anthony? What's going on?"

"I'm outta here, man."

"What do you mean, you're outta here? What's wrong?"

"Yeah, well, first you lead 'em right to Gant so they can kill his ass right in front of his family. Then you tell the cops about me. Like I say, I'm outta here."

"Hold on, Anthony. I didn't lead anybody anywhere. I've been very careful about that. And I certainly haven't said anything about you to the cops. Why would you even think I would do that?"

"Cause you just said you did. On TV. You said you told 'em the truth 'bout why you went talkin' to Gant."

Frank wagged his head woefully. "Anthony, I had to say that to get the fuckin' papers off my back. Fact is I haven't mentioned you or the details of your story to anyone, not even here at the station. So cool out, man."

"Yeah, so you cool out. Cause I'm splittin'. I'm leavin' this fuckin' town while I'm still breathin', and you can forget ever seein' me again."

"Anthony, wait..."

He heard nothing but dial tone.

Chapter 49

Frank found Letty Pell's condo on the top floor of the Riverfront Towers, a high-end high-rise downtown on the river. She met him at the door with a glass of Merlot, maybe the tightest jeans he'd ever seen, a wonderfully skimpy top and a cascade of wild red curls. Settled on her plush cream leather couch, she lifted her own wine glass, clinked the one she had handed him and said, "Cheers!"

After their initial sips, she reached for his belt, and he surprised both of them by taking her hand and bringing it to his lips before saying, "Hey, let's wait just a bit."

She smiled kindly. "Whatever you'd like. I just thought you looked a little tense on TV. That's why I called. That and the fact that you haven't called me."

So why had he not called her, and why stop her now? Certainly not because she had oversold her talent. If anything, she had been too modest. Was he getting paranoid? Maybe, since the thought had occurred that perhaps Judge Billy was behind her phoned invitation. Get a closer look and report her observations. Now even their initial encounter, way back at the Economic Club, seemed suspicious. Too good to be truly accidental?

From the looks of this place, for a gal who claimed she didn't work for a living, she was clearly on good terms with someone of means. "Nice little pad you got here, Letty."

"Why, thank you, kind sir. I enjoy it. But it's been a little lonely lately, waiting for you to call. I've missed you!"

"Letty, please. With your looks and talents, you must have all the town's movers and shakers lined up around the block."

"What a nice and naughty thing to say. But really, Frank, I've been surprised and disappointed you haven't called me. I thought we hit it off so well, and nobody takes me to the classy places you do."

Frank gave her a grin while he thought about how quickly she had brought up the dive where he had tried to chase down Randal

Byrd. "Well, I've been swamped with work lately."

"Yeah? Well, tell me, did you ever catch up with that weird guy you were chasing that night. What was his name? Randal Rat?"

He laughed, searching her glinting brown eyes, as if he might fathom there why she was asking the question. "No, Byrd, Randal Byrd. I've had no luck on that one."

"Well, what about—and now I'm going to show you that I really do watch you all the time—what about the poor guy whose family got blown up in their car? What's his name? Person or something like that? You were asking him to call practically every night there for a while. Did he ever call you? And are we ever going to learn why that awful thing happened?"

She certainly wasn't wasting any time. And those were nice little touches, changing Byrd to Rat and not getting Anthony's name right either.

"No, sorry, I've struck out on that one too."

"Well, then how's your book coming?"

"Oh, thanks for asking. Ah, little by little. You know, I told you it's a labor of love. And with so much on my plate, it kind of gets short shrift."

"That's too bad, but just remember, when you finish, I definitely want to read it."

He gazed steadily at her. The woman was certainly trying to push every button. "That's very sweet of you to say, Letty. But talking about guys lining up around the block for you, I wonder if you might know an old friend of mine, Judge William J. O'Bryan? You know Billy, by any chance?"

Did the sparkling brown eyes flicker for an instant? He was not really sure. "No, I can't say that I do. Should I?"

"Oh, yes, Billy's quite the charmer. Hell of a ladies man, in the sense that he adores women and seems to know how to please them. Yeah, you should ring him up at the courthouse. Just leave word that I suggested you call, and he'll get right back to you, if I know Billy."

She took his hand and put it on her thigh. "Well, thanks for the tip. But why are we talking about other guys when I've got the guy I want right here on my couch?"

Chapter 50

Anthony Peoples had been to Cleveland one other time. Back when they were both still in their teens, he and his cousin Rick had driven to the city in Anthony's rickety Escort wagon, the only vehicle they had between them at the time, and against the firmly stated wishes of Juanita, who had thought he should have nothing to do with a "dangerous personality" like Rick.

Even back then, Anthony had harbored no doubt that his childhood sweetheart meant salvation from the street. Without Nita he would certainly have been running with Rick and most likely losing himself in a dead-end life. But Rick had asked him for a ride to Cleveland to see a girl he had met at a Run DMC concert a few weeks earlier, and Anthony had felt like it was something he just had to do, both for Rick and to show Nita he had a mind of his own.

It had been the last trip the once "best cousins" had ever taken together, and afterward each had begun to find his own way.

For Rick, strictly "Pretty Rick" back then, and strictly small-time, dealing junk and the occasional whore on Detroit's near westside, the break had come when the girl from Cleveland had hooked him up with her half-sister who just happened to be running an outfit supplying half the stuff in that old Pingree Street neighborhood. The half-sister had been looking for some smart muscle, "heady pop" she had called it, and Rick, despite his slight build and effeminate style, had heady pop to spare. Within a year he had his first Maserati, a four-year-old BiTurbo coupe. And two years and three Maseratis later, with the half-sister suffering an advanced case of AIDS, he had been running the show.

Actually, the show had turned out to be a wholly-owned subsidiary of the Monelli clan. And for a time, with his love of Italian cars and the Monellis' need for efficient street operations, "Maserati Rick" Mahone had thought it was a marriage made in heaven. Eventually, like everything else in this world, that had changed.

As for Anthony, with Nita's prodding, pleading and homework help, he had managed to get through a year and a half at Wayne County Community College. A job as an investigator with the city's water department had followed, dealing with residents' complaints. Actually he had enjoyed the work and for a time thought he might have a future with the department. There had been posts in the upper echelon he felt he could qualify for eventually, perhaps with a little more college.

He and Nita had married and started a family; they had bought a small home on the city's southwest side and had generally lived on his salary while putting most of hers from the bank in a saving's account and a couple of conservative mutual funds. Life had seemed good. Certainly he had no regrets about leaving Rick to his risked-filled career.

Then the city had hit a particularly rough patch, and layoffs in the water departments had sent him home without a job. By then, with Damon three and a half and Sara 16 months, Anthony and Nita had agreed that, rather than taking just any job, he should stay home with the kids, save on child care, take some night classes and wait for the right opportunity.

In the ensuing years, Anthony and Rick had seen each other only occasionally, usually at some family function. A wedding, a funeral, the big annual summer picnic always on Belle Isle, the city's major park in the middle of the Detroit River. But the meetings had become much less frequent, and their last time together had been at Anthony's sister's wedding, a year before Anthony's trouble with the law. By then Rick had been on his sixth Maserati, and despite each man's effort to keep his demeanor casual, there had been an uncomfortable stiffness about their attempts at conversation.

The fact that many in the family at this happy affair had been fawning on Rick hadn't helped. But several months later when Anthony had been charged with murder, Rick neither hesitated nor asked. He had simply ordered Sam Dworkin to call his cousin and announce he was taking on the case.

And while Nita had been certain it would be much wiser for Anthony to find his own lawyer, this had been another of those rare moments when Anthony had known that to be his own man, he would have to defy his wife.

Chapter 51

Anthony's big sister Vanessa, who worked for the postal service, married a man originally from Kashmir. It was a whirlwind romance, four weeks and they were married. He said he was a doctor with a practice in Cleveland, but when the newlyweds arrived there, it turned out the man was actually a failing second-year med student at Case Western Reserve. Even so, Vanessa, who had transfered to a job at Cleveland's main post office, bought a bungalow for them in the Glenville neighborhood near the lake. Five months later she came home one day to find all her husband's clothes and belongings gone.

"So how you settlin' in?" she asked Anthony as he sampled her spicy gumbo, one of his favorites. Sitting at a small kitchen table, she watched her baby brother give a half-nod with a low, pleasant moan.

She had told him he was welcome to stay in her spare bedroom as long as he liked. But after a week now, he could not bring himself to say the truth: he had no intention of staying. He was reasonably sure the local cops, the ones who had checked out Vanessa that first week he went missing, wouldn't be back soon, but she was putting herself at risk by taking him in. He had sworn he would never again jeopardize anyone else he loved. So he said only that he felt very comfortable, thanks to her, and he would be eternally grateful.

"Anthony, I'm your sister for godsake. Why didn't you come to me in the first place?"

"Ness, I told you, cause I was feelin' safer hidin' in broad daylight in the middle of a city I know better'n any place else. And there was also a guy that helped me. You knew him back in the day. DeShawn gave me a little loan, and then he was leavin' for a trip to see his family, drivin' down to Baton Rouge. I gave him some plastic, my bankcard and a Visa, asked him to get me some cash on the way down and use the Visa for some things when he got there."

"You wanted them thinkin' you left for down there. Good, Anthony."

He shook his head. "Ness, you don't know these people I'm dealing with and what they're capable of. I didn't want to bring all that to you. Still don't."

Vanessa eyed him silently for a moment. Then she spoke softly. "I haven't asked you what happened that day. I wanted you to know I believe in you without question. I know it must be too painful to even hold in your mind. But if you ever feel like you want to, or can, I hope you will talk to me about it."

He said after a moment, "I can talk about it."

She looked down at her gumbo. "Okay, so first, tell me what happened to Rick. I mean I read the stories in the paper you sent me. But what really happened? You pick up anything from his friends, or on the street?"

"I picked up a little on the street, and I know this one boy was really tight with him. I was also going to night school with this other guy who's a cop, so I heard some things. Turns out our little Rick was about to be makin' a big score. I mean real big. Somehow or other—I heard it was through some spic dude he got to knowin' in L.A.—he was about to make his own direct connect with some Mexican pipeline. And this made these big Eye-talian dudes very pissed off. Word on the street was they got him."

Vanessa shook her head. "But Ricky was nothin' but smart. He musta known they'd be after him. Why would he let them even get close?"

"Ness, when they want to do you, they got their ways, man. Anyhow, this courtesy car driving the freeway at two in the morning come up on this big Maserati—Quadroporte, I think—parked on the shoulder on I-75. They stop and the car's still running, and Rick's behind the wheel with his head back against the headrest. Like he just stopped and pulled over and takin' a nap. 'Cept there's this little hole just above his nose. And later they find this other one just behind his ear."

"You go to the funeral?"

"Yeah."

"Was it bad like they said in the paper?"

"Pretty bad. Like Nita said, they coulda fed half the city with what they dropped on it. This big, custom-made casket made outta parts from that first Maserati he owned. Bumpers in the front and back, wheels, part of the engine and inside a steering wheel and part of the

106

dashboard. He's lying there like he's sleepin' behind the wheel, just like when they found him on the freeway.

"I spent the whole time in front of the casket not thinking about when we were eight and we'd walk to grandma's house and get eggnog after school, and how he stood up for me, even though he was so much smaller than me, when these older dudes tried to shake me down. I just kept trying to see where the bullet holes were."

"Sad."

"Way sad."

Silent for a while, Vanessa finally said, "So, Anthony, tell what happened with the bomb. If you feel like you can."

He said, "Well, but look, okay, when I was hidin' back there, I talked to Gant on the phone, just like a week before they popped him. And I only know what he told me, true or not."

"Which was?"

"Which was somehow they found out about the tape and stuff. He figured somebody in his office sang. And he was bein' squeezed to drop the whole thing."

"Yes."

"But back then I didn't know none of this."

"Right."

"So that morning I get this call from Gant sayin' there's this big change in the case, and he needs me to come in right away and with the tape."

"Your copy."

"Yeah, my copy. But I say, 'Well, but I told you I'm goin' today to Chi-town with Nita and the kids to her sister's.' And he says, flat out, 'No, you're not doin' that! You have Nita take the kids and go. Be better for them out of town anyways. And you come on down here to my office at the courthouse at 7 pm. You got no choice.'

"So we're plannin' to take the Caravan, but that damn piece-a-shit been stallin' so much I took it in to the shop that morning. They say it need a fuel pump, and they can't get one 'til Monday, so they need to keep it. Nita says, 'It's okay, you take us to the Amtrak, and we'll take the train. Be the first time for the kids. They'll love it.' So that's the plan. I'll drive 'em to the Amtrak in my car, and then I'll meet with Gant.

"But Nita don't know 'bout the tape. She just know if the prosecutor say, 'Jump,' I gotta jump. So we're runnin' late. I already

107

got the suitcase in the Dodge, and I tell her to take the kids out there and get it started, and I'll be right there. I'm gettin' the tape where I have it stashed behind the furnace in the basement. And I hear the bomb. And feel it. It shook stuff all over the basement. By the time I'm upstairs lookin' out the window, Nita and the babies..."

He stopped. After a few seconds he opened his mouth, but he couldn't speak.

Vanessa covered his hand with hers and said in a whisper, "Baby, don't."

Glancing at his sister, he saw tears rolling on her cheeks. He looked away and said, " I ain't gonna cry. I cried enough. Some way they gonna pay."

Chapter 52

"Nice ball, Billy." Frank watched the judge's drive tail a bit before bounding on the bright green fairway and finally roll to a stop on the right edge about 240 out. Picking up his tee, the judge made a little move with his hips that Frank knew was meant to ward off a slice. Having played together since high school, they knew each other's game almost as well as their own. O'Bryan climbed into the cart, and they headed down this lush fairway at beautiful Oakland Hills.

The site of major championships over the years and the area's premier private club, it's $25,000 annual membership fee had been part of Frank's last two contracts with WTEM.

With his ball up the left side about ten yards beyond the judge, they rolled up to Billy's ball first, and Frank wondered how long it had been since he'd seen his best friend.

Was Billy really his best friend? If not, then who? That racket ball game had been over a month ago now, and they had talked only briefly on the phone since.

Chit-chat over the first few holes had covered the easy stuff — kids and family items. The judge had been out of town for two weeks. As usual he and Gloria had opened their lakefront home up north for the summer. Gloria, 19-year-old Cindy and little Missy would spend much of the season up there. Billy and 22-year-old Martin, who was interning at a large firm in the city before heading off to law school at Michigan, would commute often on the weekends.

Billy hit a 7-iron over the green on the right, and Frank said nothing as he drove them back across the fairway to his ball. At 50 bucks a hole, this game was just as competitive as their racket ball. As he pulled out his 8-iron, he said, "Well, you left it wide open for me, your honor."

"Just testing your nerve."

Frank hit it on line but barely made the front of the green, leaving himself a long uphill putt. He could already hear Billy saying "Never up, never in," but the judge changed the subject.

"So, Frankie, what were you really doing that night visiting Prentis Gant?"

He had been waiting for this. "Just what I said I was doing, what I told the cops and everybody else on the news. Were you watching?"

"Oh, yeah, but I mean beyond the stuff about asking him why he resigned. We both know you didn't go to his place at midnight just to ask about that."

Frank had two baits ready to toss. "Hey, I got a real scoop outta that visit. Before he was murdered, Gant told me he'd been pressured to step down."

With a side glance to catch Billy's response to this double cast, he wondered which bait his friend would rise to first.

"Pressured, eh. Pressured how, and why didn't you report that?"

Frank stopped the cart near the green, got out and pulled his putter. "Hey, I never tell everything I know. In any case, he didn't say. He just said he'd been forced to step down and that he couldn't talk about it. Yet. He said he was working on things, and there would come a time when he would talk about it. Of course, now that time will never come."

Frank had a fifty footer and the judge a long downhill chip and run. As he walked up to his ball, Billy said, "And you said 'murdered.' Everything I hear out of the prosecutor's office says suicide."

"My theory is murder."

"Your theory."

"Right. As I told the cops, from what I saw that night, he was not a man on the verge of ending it all."

"Maybe you freaked him enough to push him over the edge."

"Oh, he was freaked all right, but not by me."

"By who then?"

"By whoever was pressuring him. You got any ideas?"

The judge was over his chip now. "Why would I have any ideas?"

Frank kibbitzed. "Careful, you give that a little bit too much, you're gonna be right down here with me."

"Thanks for the advice, pal."

The judge rolled his chip well past the hole and missed coming back. Frank managed to get down in two, and now he was 150 bucks up.

Moving to the next tee, the judge again changed the subject. "By the way, you ever hear from that guy who lost his wife and kids in that car bomb? The one you keep asking to call you?"

Time for more invention. "No, I sure wish I had. Probably skipped town. You pick up any gossip about him or that bomb?"

"The cops I talk to think he probably did it himself."

Frank's response had a bit more heat than he wanted. "Why the fuck would he do that?"

Billy looked at him for a couple of seconds. "Why do evil or fucked up people do any of the things they do? Because they're evil or fucked up."

At the next tee, they both pulled their drivers, and Frank said casually, "Well, on a much more pleasant topic, have you heard from a friend of mine named Letty Pell? Lots of red curls, a great body and a very special talent I know you'd enjoy."

Stopping his set up, he gazed at Billy's face. As usual it betrayed nothing.

"No, but it sounds like I'd appreciate her call."

Chapter 53

"So what's going on with your mom?"

Hoping to catch a clue, he glanced at his daughter's hazel eyes, her mother's eyes, as he twirled with a fork the fettucini with a diced sausage sauce he had almost every time he came here to the Roma, the city's oldest Italian place.

The quick little frown Jennie tried to hide did not bode well. "Meaning is she still talking about the divorce thing?"

"Yeah, the divorce thing," said Frank. "Did she really hire Hartzell?"

Bennett Hartzell was the town's toughest divorce attorney.

"I don't know, but she sounds pretty matter of fact, like it's gonna happen."

"Well, at least she hasn't called off our trip to the island next week, right?"

"Right."

"She say anything about it?"

"Only that we can all live together just as easily in the Provo house as we can here. Even with a split pending."

With a nod he stuffed a wad of rolled up pasta in his mouth.

Jennie said, "Daddy, can I ask you something?"

"Ask away."

"Did you invite me to dinner just to spy on Mom?"

He swallowed and tried not to look offended, a sure sign of guilt. "No way."

"Because you didn't need to. You should know by now I'm totally on your side."

She was looking at him so earnestly, that scooped neckline showing so much of her lovely top that he felt almost uncomfortable with his own daughter. He wanted to tell this sweet, smart and sexy girl not to worry about her womanly allure, but he needed to find a fatherly way to say it.

"I know that, baby, and I appreciate it. I called because I feel like I haven't seen much of you this summer, and I realized, when we had

112

that chat a while back down by the lake, that I really didn't know much about what you're thinking and feeling these days. I used to be able to tell just by looking at you, but it seems like overnight you've become this mature young woman, with all the wonderful mystery of your sex, and I can't seem to tell anymore."

"Daddy, stop bullshitting."

"I'm not bullshitting. Why does everyone think I'm bullshitting?"

"Because we all know how good you are at it."

Frank shook his head. "Well, anyway, I just think before we know it, you'll be heading back to U. of M., and then it'll be even tougher to know how you are and what you're up to."

"Yeah, well, I'm not sure I'm gonna want you to know what I'm up to."

Thankfully, she offered this with a small mischievous smile.

"Jen, you know what I mean. I'm not your mom. I just want to know how you're doing in class and with your writing, that kind of thing. I mean last year you suddenly started talking about quitting school and spending your time writing a novel in iambic pentameter or some damn thing. I want to know about these things, so I can be a father and give you all the wrong advice."

"It was an epic poem in free verse, and I thought your advice was pretty good. That's why I decided not to do it."

"Really? What'd I say?"

"You said you thought it was an admirable ambition, but why not finish the year and really learn other poetic styles, like iambic pentameter, because otherwise writing free verse is like playing tennis with the net down. And then this summer if I still wanted to do it, you'd send me to Spain or France or wherever I wanted to go, and I could write it there."

"Okay, so what *have* you been writing this summer?"

"A few poems, but mostly short stories. I've just fallen in love with that form. It's just this fantastic combination of freedom and discipline."

Now that he was gazing at a new light in those hazel eyes, he felt a lift. "So I hope I can read one soon."

"Of course, but how about you, Daddy. How's the book coming? 'Buffaloes in the City.' I love that title."

"Well, I haven't been able to work on it much lately, but this morning I finished a chapter called 'Smear Monday Romance.'"

"Smear was a card game, right?"

"And Smear Monday is the day after Easter. Anyway it's the story of Marcel Sutterman and Margaret DeValkeneeer and how they got together back in 1924."

"So how did Marcel and Margaret get together?"

He was pleased she wanted to know, or at least that she asked. "Well, he's this big, strapping 20-year-old kid who at 15 had somehow found his way from Brussels to this little town on Superior where he got a job mining iron ore. On Easter Sunday he goes to St. Anthony's Church and spots this beautiful young girl. He can't take his eyes off her, but even though she smiles at him in the church, he's too shy to go up to her after the service.

"Anyway, the next day, Smear Monday, as was the custom, all the men gather at the Belgian Club in an old saloon to play lots of cards and drink lots of beer. After a while, and probably way too much beer, he's still day-dreaming about this girl and not paying attention to his cards, and his partner gets so pissed that he starts a fight with him. It quickly turns into a free-for-all, Marcel ends up getting blind-sided by a guy whacking him over the head with a chair. He's out like a light and they have to take him to the little hospital in town.

"When he finally wakes up, he thinks he's dead because this angel in white is standing there, looking just like the gal he'd been staring at in church. So, of course, the nurse is Margaret. She's 16, one of ten kids, most of them born here to this Flemish couple from a little coastal town in the old country. Marcel's got a nasty gash in his forehead and a concussion, and she nurses him back to health. He's so shy that when she has to give him a bath in bed, he keeps his eyes closed the whole time. Within eight months they're married.

"They end up having five kids and when the mine slows down and he loses his job, he moves the whole family down here where the plants are hiring. Four of the five kids are college graduates and the fifth takes his father's job in the plant. Margaret told me their story a few months back and said six years ago, after 62 years of marriage, Marcel died in her arms while they were...you know."

"My god, and he was what, in his eighties?"

"Yep. You know what they say about us Flemish guys."

"Yeah, well, wow, what a great story."

Frank saw her gaze move from him to something over his left shoulder, and now from behind came an uncomfortably familiar voice.

"So this must be where you take all your mistresses."

He turned to find Sherie looking radiantly angry in a devastating red dress.

"Hey, Frank. Fancy meeting you here, the place we first met. Remember, Frank, right over there at the bar where you picked me up? And surely you recall our favorite booth over there to the left, where we'd always sit, back when you still had the time and interest to take me out to dinner. We haven't been here in so long that I had to come and remind myself why I loved it so much. And what do I find, but my Frankie boy with his latest bimbette."

She had't taken her eyes off him but turned now to give her full attention to Jennie.

"Sweetie, you look a little young even for this self-enchanted prick. So let me tell you where all this is heading, and then you can decide whether you really want to go there. Right now, I'm sure, though self-obsessed, he's totally charming. He's attentive, sensitive to your every little need, and, it goes without saying, a dynamite lover. Today you're enthralled with his stories, but I can tell you they'll get old. For a while you'll feel like the most important thing in his universe, and then one day it'll seem like he's moved on to another galaxy. And the only time he'll show his face is in that box sitting on your TV stand. So, honey, do yourself a favor. Turn him off and pull the plug."

She turned back with a pissed-off smile to see how he was taking this. Quietly he said, "Sherie Sloan meet my daughter Jennifer."

The smile melted badly as she glanced back at Jennie. Then not quite looking him in the eye, she said softly, "Sorry, Frank."

As she walked away, he watched her gorgeous ass moving exactly as it did the first time he saw her, heading from the bar to the ladies room that night two years ago.

Turning back to Jennie, he found her with a placid look. "Daddy, can you even imagine being married to the same person for 62 years?"

There had been many times since that stunning moment he had first seen her, a lovely, wrinkled infant just out of Marci's body, that he had felt hopelessly in love with his daughter.

Never, he thought, had he ever loved her quite as much as he did right now.

Chapter 54

"Hey, Fay, got a sec?"

On her way to Frank's office, she looked up to find Mary Scott, holding a sheet of paper next to that push-button smile of hers.

"Hi, Mary. Sure, what's up?"

Just about everything about this woman drove her nuts, her name, her clothes, her church, everything. And yet they were both single black women in their early 30s, both attractive, neat, efficient. So was this some kind of projected self-hatred? She really didn't think so.

Mary handed her the sheet of paper. "I just pulled this off the wire. The Supreme Court has upheld parts of a Pennsylvania law imposing some limits on a woman's ability to obtain an abortion. President Bush, of course, has issued a statement saying again he opposes abortion in all cases except rape or incest or where the life of the mother is at stake. Clinton, of course, is singing his same old tired song about Roe v. Wade."

Fay said, "Of course," but thought, "As usual, bitch, you feel the need to demonstrate your full grasp of the story even with me here in a back hallway." Depending on her mood, Mary treated her as either a victim or a traitor. A victim to be pitied for working with the Enemy. Or a traitor to her race and gender to be scorned and despised for working with the Enemy.

Mary said, "Well, I just really want to read this story tonight. I think I should read this story tonight. I mean, a woman should read this story."

"Why are you saying this to me?"

"Why? Because this is a woman's story. With a powerful impact on women's lives."

"No, I mean why aren't you talking about this with Dennis? He's the show producer."

"Oh, I will. But Dennis doesn't matter." A dismissive flip of her hand. "He'll say yes, and then Frank will raise his little finger, and

116

Dennis will cave. It always happens."

"So you want me to say something to Frank."

"Would you? Oh, thank you so much, Fay. This means a lot to me."

"No problem. I'll talk to him right now."

Fay handed back the sheet and walked away, thinking, "Okay, Fatima."

She was the only one at the station who knew the woman's real name: Fatima Rolling. Info picked up on a flight to D.C. last year from a seatmate who went to grade school with little Fatima back in Gary. So obviously the woman had chosen the whitest name she could think of. Dressed like the prissiest white girl, always buttoned up, always with those slacks or a pants suit. And she knew why Fatima really wanted to read that story. Because it would please all those good Christian folks at her church, that mostly white World of Faith crowd, where wealth and success are the surest signs of God's favor.

Fay had never even told Frank about Mary Scott's real name. Those two already had enough going on without handing him a juicy little item that he could probably not resist using. She knew Frank well, including most of his demons and his frailties. She also liked and admired him. Actually, there was part of her that was almost disappointed he'd never come on to her. Almost.

The most important thing: he had always treated her with professional respect and a kind of paternal affection. Bottom line, he was not just smart, but clever and intuitive about people, dedicated, caring and, probably more than any white guy she had ever known, color blind.

In his office, he was lounging at his desk looking at a magazine from Providenciales, that Caribbean island where he owned a home. She asked, "So when do you leave?"

"Sunday morning."

"You fly to Miami and then...?"

"Just an hour and a quarter. It's one of the reasons we built down there."

"I just ran into Queen of." Their pet name for her, as in Mary, Queen of Scots.

"Yeah." He was not interested.

"She wants to read the story on the Supremes and abortion."

"Why?"

"It's not worth going into. Just say yes."

"It's not my call."

"She thinks it is."

"Okay then, yes."

Chapter 55

Sprawled, spent, his body still tingling, he finally turned in the bed and gently turned her with him until their bodies were spooning, his arm around her, his hand curled gently around her warm, moist breast.

He said softly, "'Self-enchanted prick,' I think that was my favorite line."

She laughed. "Really? I thought that was pretty good myself."

"Oh, yeah, that was good. But I was impressed with the whole damn speech. You were really on your game. Poor Jen will probably never forget that moment, which is actually good because you were saying things that every attractive young woman should probably hear."

"Yeah, well, when you told me who she was, I thought, so, okay, I'll never see him again."

"Oh, god, no, I wanted you more than ever after that."

He caressed her breast and she turned her head so he could kiss her warm, full lips.

He couldn't recall who told him—maybe 30 years ago when he was somewhere in his teens, the advice lodged securely in some corner of his memory ever since—that nurses were typically sensual and good in bed. Certainly this young woman, with an amazingly soft touch and an astonishing ability to stoke and revel in her own pleasure, pleased him sexually, as much or more than anyone ever had. Was it four or five times she came? He couldn't tell because at one point she had orgasmed for so long he thought she must have stopped for a while and then started again.

So why had he called her to say, "How about dinner and a movie?" Something he hadn't done in months. Because he wanted, needed another taste of her reliable rapture? Or because he was worried about what she might do while he was off in the Caribbean with his family? Like talk to Wil Barnes? No doubt both.

For the first time in months he had pulled the Caddy with the heavily tinted windows out of the garage and left the Viper in its place. And as they had walked to it coming out of her apartment building she had said, "Ah, going incognito tonight."

"Yeah, busted. With what's been in the papers lately and with that little bitch Barnes working with his spies all over town, I thought it was a good idea."

Nodding silently, she had slipped into the plush interior with its soft leather seats, no doubt knowing bloody well why he had mentioned Barnes and spies. Still, with him seated behind the wheel, she had reached to caress his face, kissed him on the mouth and said, "I've missed you so much, Frank."

"I've missed you too." He had said it even though his life had felt way too crazed and complicated to miss anyone.

On the way to the movie he had asked if she'd mind if they saw "The Player." No, but what happened to "Batman Returns." His mood had shifted, he said. He wanted less bombast and more intelligence. He had read great reviews and had loved Altman ever since "McCabe and Mrs. Miller."

On their arriaval, she had asked if his choice might have anything to do with "The Player" showing at a small, quiet 3-screen theater and Batman playing at a large, bustling multiplex. As they left the Cadillac, he had slipped on a pair of black sunglasses and said, no way. Taking his arm as they walked through the lot, she had hugged it anyway.

Later on the way to dinner he had pulled another switch. Having mentioned the Roma, he had instead announced a yen for Chinese and would the Green Lantern be okay? A tiny place in an out of the way strip mall. She had said simply that she doubted little Wong Li and his wife were acquainted with Wil Barnes.

Even though she had called him on every one of his little maneuvers, her warmth and smiles had flowed as they savored the Silver Needle Noodle Chicken and chewed over "The Player." Finishing the meal, he had told her something new: he, Marci and the kids were leaving tomorrow morning and spending nine days together at their home on Provo.

She had looked down at her green mint ice cream and still-unopened fortune cookie and said nothing. Then he had said that Marci had told him recently that she was divorcing him.

Her blue eyes, large and lovely, came up from the ice cream, and after a moment she asked softly, "Is she really going to do that?"

"I don't know, but she says she's already hired the best divorce attorney in town."

"Well, how do you feel about that?"

Saying nothing for a few seconds, he had wanted to be truthful but wanted more to say anything that would encourage her not to talk to the despicable Mr. Barnes. Finally, gazing at the bald little Wong Li behind the cash register, he had said, "I don't know. I'm kind of numb I guess. I always thought I'd be the instigator, but now it's kind of out of my hands. I guess I'm worried about the kids."

She said gently, "Well, they're both basically adults, Frank."

"Yeah, you're right. But to me they're still kids."

"They'll be all right. Kids are a lot stronger than we give them credit for."

She had sounded like the divorce was already a sure thing. Best to leave it at that. Picking up his fortune cookie, he had broken it open. "'You value constancy and a good heart above all.'" He crumpled the little slip of white paper and tossed it on the table. "I hate these non-fortune fortune cookies."

"Well, no, that is a fortune, if you believe that character is fate."

He had smiled. "Open yours."

Cracking the cookie, she had gazed at the little white strip, her beautiful mouth forming a smile. "'Soon your fondest dream will come true.'"

"No. You're making that up."

"I'm not. Look for yourself." She had handed it to him.

"Well, I'll be. 'Soon your fondest dream will come true.' Okay, what's your fondest dream?"

She had looked at him directly and said, "I'm not telling."

Now in her bed she turned her body to him with such a sexy twist that he felt himself getting hard again. She said, "So if she's getting a divorce, why is she going away with you for 10 days?"

"Nine days. I don't know. She says it's for the kids."

Sherie stared at him, and he already knew what was coming. "Frank, you're such a bullshitter."

Chapter 56

At Jimmy's on the Beach on Grace Bay, a rustic old bar carved out of the remains of an abandoned motel and restaurant, they clinked their Coronas with the slice of lime still protruding from each rim. "To a great day on the links. May we enjoy another very soon."

"I'll drink to that," said Bobby, squeezing and pushing the lime wedge into his bottle.

Frank raised his bottle again. "And to a great senior year comin' up, with lots of success and good times ahead."

Bobby stared at his bottle. "I don't know if I'm drinking to that."

"Why not?" said Frank, looking away at the powdery white sand and the brilliant, surreal greens and blues stretching to the horizon, interrupted only by a line of white caps caused by the huge unspoiled reef a mile out, a view that never failed to lift his mood. "How can you not drink to good times?"

"Yeah, good times are cool. But I'm not sure I want a successful senior year, at least in terms of how the good fathers see it."

"What's wrong with how they see it?" Frank stared back at his son, who in turn gazed at the sea and took a swig.

"For them success is all about grades and the right extra-curriculars, to get you a slot at the right college, that'll insure the right career path, that'll lead to the right retirement package, that'll tide you over until you slide into the right afterlife community."

When Bobby glanced at him to see how that little gambit had gone over, Frank nodded. "'The right afterlife community.' I kind of like that."

"It's yours, no charge."

"Hey, thanks, kiddo." Frank saw Bobby's mild smile turn almost imperceptibly to a faint frown and realized he hadn't called this son kiddo in years. Kiddo had always been Tommy, and on the rare occasion when he'd used it for Bobby, it had felt almost like a slip.

Rare occasions. Surely this day was one. It had started with the two of them having breakfast on the deck at the back of the house, sitting high on a bluff looking out at the open Caribbean to the south.

As usual, he had seen little of his family in these first few days on Provo, with Marci sticking close to home, working on her decorating projects, the kids spending most of their time on the water, using the skiff to meet up with friends to fish and snorkel. His own routine was to hit the links on the island's lone golf course in the morning, then tinker around the house or drive over to Long Bay Beach and walk naked in the brilliant sun.

Bobby was perfectly capable these days of sitting alone with his father for a half-hour and, except for a "Hi" and a "See ya," never utter a word. This morning, though, his son had caught him gazing mindlessly across the bay at Dick Clark's big house and asked, "Did you ever meet him."

Frank had been startled by his son's voice. "Meet who?"

"Clark. You were staring at his house."

"Oh, was I? Yeah, once. Last year at the Caicos Café. He was with Washington Misick, the chief minister, who apparently told him something about me, because Clark came over and introduced himself and said welcome to the island, I hear we're neighbors, that kind of thing."

"So what was he like?"

"He was very nice, down to earth, just seemed like a regular guy."

"So just like he is on New Year's Rockin' Eve."

"Yeah, pretty much. He seemed more interested in me than I was in him."

"Maybe he's gay."

"I didn't mean it that way."

"I know. I was just pulling your chain."

Frank had nodded and then figured nothing ventured, nothing gained: "So how about a round with me this morning?"

Bobby had waited for a couple of seconds, then said lightly, "Okay. But no betting. I just want to play."

"Great."

"And I want to beat your ass."

"Well, okay then. Let's get it on."

At the course they had played together for the first time in over a year, since before Tommy's death. Just the two of them, except for the last two holes on the front nine when they had overtaken a couple of old codgers playing for heavy stakes and cheating whenever possible. With one look at Bobby, tall, lots of sandy hair, a trim, athletic physique, they had started gushing. The kid had "one helluva sweet swing." And could be "turnin' pro tomorrow if you want it."

Leaving the old farts at the clubhouse, they had moved on to the back nine, Bobby saying quietly, "Couple of old bullshitters."

"They weren't just being nice to you. They really were impressed with your swing."

"But you see them cheating their asses off?"

"That's just part of the game for them. Makes it more interesting."

"You're probably right. I never thought of it that way."

Frank and his son had played even until eighteen, where Frank had missed a six-footer to give Bobby the match.

"You pushed that on purpose."

"The hell I did. You beat me fair and square."

"That was a flat, straight-in putt. You make those in your sleep."

"Well, as you know, I'm fully capable of all manner of fuck-ups and mistakes. Besides, you played damned well for somebody who hasn't touched a club in two months."

Now at Jimmy's he searched for something witty and wise to offer his son on the pursuit of success. Then he thought about how fiercely competitive the boy had been on the course and decided to let it go.

Instead, he said, "You know, Bobby, I'm afraid I owe you an apology."

The boy's brown eyes turned curious. "For what?"

"Well, for kind of ignoring you for the past several months. I've been more or less stuck in my own grief, and when I did manage to think about someone else, I'm afraid I paid more attention to Jen because she just seemed crushed by what happened, for obvious reasons. I don't think I've been much good for your mom either."

Bobby's look was almost defiant. "Mom's strong."

He smiled sadly at his son. "Yes, she is. Very strong. But no mother should have to go through something like that. It's just horribly unfair."

He paused as Bobby dropped his gaze to the heavily scarred old table top between them. "Anyway, I just thought an apology was in order, and I hope you'll accept it."

Bobby looked up and said, "No apology needed. I'm okay. I'm

strong too, and I'll do okay."

Frank nodded. "Yeah, I'm sure you will."

He stared at the incredible colors of the endless sea in front of him and somehow thought of the little lake behind their home in Bloomfield Hills. And he thought of that day last August, the one he could almost never bring himself to think about. That day when Jen's hysterical screams and Bobby's desperate calls, "Dad! Dad!!" had brought them, frantic, out of the house and onto the deck.

He had sprinted ahead of Marci down the slope to the dock where Tommy's lifeless body was splayed. One sickening look at all the blood and the bits of brain tissue oozing out of that huge gash in his right forehead, and he knew it was already over.

There had been only one thought at that point: don't let Marci see this. He had grabbed Bobby roughly by the arm and dragged him to the foot of the dock where he caught Marci running at full tilt, stopped her and with Bobby turned her back toward the house, yelling at them, "Call 911. The cops and EMS."

Moving back down the dock he had found Jen on her knees, her terrified screams animal-like, trying to push the blood and tissue back into that gaping wound and close it somehow. For a moment he had thought he was going to vomit.

But he did not. And he did not disintegrate into a thousand pieces or stop breathing, or any of the things he had always thought would happen if something truly awful struck down one of his beautiful, precious kids. Instead he lifted his daughter to her feet and held her, weeping and shaking, in his arms.

So why in all these shit-caked days since had he never understood that Bobby, sitting here trying to feel strong, needed the same thing? Maybe not hugs, with our phoney masculine insistence on stand-alone strength, but surely, at the very least, an insistent effort to find the right moves to comfort and console.

Chapter 57

Parked in front of Cleveland's main post office, he waited behind the wheel of his sister's Civic and watched the stream of postal workers, so many of them black, leaving the building. When he spotted Vanessa smiling goodbye to a girlfriend, he shoved his arm out the window and waved. Spotting him, she waved back and seconds later slid onto the seat next to him.

"Hey, baby."

"Hey, Ness." He turned the ignition. "How was it today?"

"Well, put it this way. Any day with no paper cuts, letter bombs, vasoline-smeared envelopes, or crazed co-workers is a blessed day. How about you?"

Getting a break in traffic, he pulled the Civic away from the curb and headed for Glenville. He had decided he might as well just go ahead with it now.

"Ness, I been thinkin' about goin' back."

She gave him a worried glance. "Back where?"

"Back. You know, go back and do the right thing. Lay it all down. Show 'em the tape and expose their asses."

As he drove, Vanessa stared at him. "'Expose their asses.' And just what do you think they're gonna do if you try to expose their asses? They're gonna kill you, Anthony. They're gonna destroy you, just like they destroyed that prosecutor who was stupid enough to think he could mess with them. They're too powerful, Anthony. They got too many connections. They'll squash you, like a bug."

"Maybe, but I got that TV guy, and I just feel I gotta do it for Nita and the babies."

"I thought you said you got no trust in the TV guy."

"Yeah, well..."

"And Nita and those babies would want only one thing. For you to live. To be real smart and live your life. That's what Nita always said, 'Be smart, Anthony. Do the smart thing.' I can still hear her sayin' it."

He stopped the car for a red light and looked at his sister. Those big eyes were even wider with concern. "And what I hear her sayin' is, 'Do the right thing, Anthony. Always do the right thing.'"

She closed those eyes for a few seconds then opened them, looking even more determined.

"Then all this is simple, 'cause the right thing sure as hell ain't gettin' your ass murdered. And that's exactly what's gonna happen if you go back there, my beautiful little brother."

Chapter 58

In a light blue golf shirt and navy slacks, Frank reached down to check the moisture in the soil around the bougainvillea climbing high on the front porch of the big frame house. The dirt, sand really, was powdery dry in his hand, but the mass of red flowers was flourishing.

It was not always easy to know how things worked on this island, but if you found and paid the right people, it usually turned out all right. The Dominicans would arrive soon to trim and water sufficiently until next week when they'd come again after the family departed.

"You ready?"

Marci was coming out the jalousied front door, and his quick surge of affection surprised him, even after last night. Sans make up, her blond hair up in a rubber band, she wore a thin white tee over a little pair of khaki shorts and sandals. As always her tanned legs looked great, but the rest of her 43-year-old body was trim and sexy as well. He had felt that same little surge a few minutes ago when he woke her to ask if she wanted the Pathfinder while he was playing golf. She opened one eye and said, "Yes, I'll take you. Just give me five minutes."

Slapping the dust off his hands, he got into the Nissan and rolled them out of the drive and past several large, well-kept homes overlooking the sea. Turning onto a heavily rutted dirt road, he knew there'd be a couple miles of weaving around washed out pot holes, bumps and ripples until he hit the smooth relief of the old two-lane black top that would get them to the golf course 15 minutes away.

Glancing down at those tanned legs next to him, he marveled again at last night. Where had that come from, all that quick heat, passion, lust and, yes, perhaps even love? For a week, each night, he had kissed her goodnight and hoped, waiting for something more than her usual roll-away in that king-sized bed and her affect-less

"Sleep well, Frank."

Then last night, after the kiss and the roll-away in the dark, nothing, not a word, until, finally, after maybe five seconds, her voice had come softly, "Hey, can a girl get another one of those?"

Turning back to her under the sheet he had known as soon as he touched her hip, everything would be different. The incredible warmth of her skin under his hand had melted all doubts, fears and hesitation. With her eager mouth turned to him, he had kissed her with everything he had, and they had been off on the best ride he could ever remember with her, better even than those sex-crazed days when they were just kids, and he was still at the radio station.

And when they had finished, saying nothing she had fallen asleep in his arms, and he had thought, "Where has that been all these years?" And "So it seems there may still be hope."

As he pulled into the lot at the course, he wanted to say something like, "Well, what got into us last night?" But he was afraid if he talked about it, he would only underscore its sad rarity in their life together and perhaps make it disappear on the breeze wafting through their open windows. So wordlessly, he leaned over and kissed her lovely mouth.

She smiled at him. "I'll be back to get you at 2. I'm having lunch with Diana at the Grace Bay Club."

"Okay, thanks for the lift," He started to open his door, then felt her hand on this forearm. Her face had a strange look that suddenly scared him.

"Frank, I don't want you to be surprised when we get back in a few days. You'll be getting a call from Ben Hartzell about financial statements. You might want to collect anything we might need from here on the island, before we leave. I'm sure it'll be a lot easier to get the stuff here and carry it back with us than try to get it from home later."

Stunned, as if he'd been wacked in the head, he nodded silently, got out of the Pathfinder and moved to the back hatch to get his clubs.

Chapter 59

"Ah," said Fay softly, "here comes Queen of."

At a 4-top, finishing a late lunch in the WTEM cafeteria, she, Dennis, Francine and Eddie were the last ones in the room when Mary Scott came through the line, picked up an ice tea and dug in her purse to pay.

Dennis with a glance: "Yeah, the smile switch is stuck on huge lately."

"What's she so happy about?" asked Eddie.

Francine offered, "I hear she's dating that Lion running back."

"No," said Dennis, "she's just ecstatic that Frank's been gone for a week."

Francine began to wave. "We should ask her to sit with us."

Fay grabbed her hand. "Don't you dare."

Mary was standing there now with her smile. "Hey, how are the troops?"

Eddie piped, "Doin' great, babe."

The others said nothing, and the co-anchor took her tea and left.

As if the past 30 seconds had never happened, Fay announced, "So my guy in the prosecutor's office says Gant has been officially ruled a suicide. They'll have a statement this afternoon."

Dennis: "Frank won't be happy."

Fay: "Frank won't be happy about a lot of things. You saw Barnes today."

Dennis: "That guy gets away with murder. Quoting his un-named police source, saying the department is re-doubling its efforts to find Anthony Peoples, that he must now be considered a fugitive…"

"'A fugitive from justice,'" added Francine.

"Right, quoting some jerk in homicide supposedly off the record, saying that Peoples is certainly acting like a guilty guy, and that he's either skipped town and on the lam, or is 'perhaps permanently indisposed.'"

Fay shook her head. "And that tease for Sunday at the end of his column. 'Stay tuned, folks, for a major expose involving one of the Motor City's favorite media stars.'"

Francine said, "Maybe we should tell Frank. I could give him a call."

Fay again grabbed her hand. "No way, Francine. Leave the guy alone and let him finish his vacation in peace. Anyway, there's not a damn thing he can do about any of this."

Chapter 60

There was something about an island, he thought, at least this island, that made you feel wonderfully separate, no longer touched by the world beyond, with all its cares, woes, wiles, passions, pressures, confusions and contra-indications.

For more than a week now, nearly every day, he had walked naked, except for sunglasses and his wedding band, on this deserted beach. Long Bay Beach was wild, raw and empty, though certainly not untouched by the crazy, careless hand of man.

Here and there the beautiful white sand offered strewn signs of humanity: a sunscreen tube, pop cans, half a rowboat, several feet of frayed rope, a few yards of bright green fishnet, most of a straw hat, the bones of a fish released too late and picked clean by gulls, a ripped seat cushion with a family of crabs living inside, three quarters of an empty picture frame, bottles of many shapes and sizes, and even more numerous conch shells, big, pink and gleaming in the brilliant sun.

The shells had been swept slowly around a nearby point from a conch farm he had read about but never visited, the slimey creatures inside harvested and their homes released to the sea to be washed up along with everything else on his favorite beach by the predictable tides.

He walked naked on this beach because it felt good, right and reasonable. The lovely warmth of the sun and the cool tingle of a light breeze on all of his skin made wearing a suit here seem silly. Beyond that, everything he had ever come up with to explain the experience had seemed clichéd. Yes, he was more than a bit of an exhibitionist, but not on this beach. No one had ever seen him here. Certainly this place made him feel totally free, open, unguarded and strangely innocent. All clichés.

A few homes stood at the far western end of the beach, maybe three miles away, but the last access road cut through the scrub to the sand was a mile and a half away, and he had never encountered a soul at this end.

Actually, though, he had a relationship of sorts with someone else who loved this beach enough to walk it as far east as he did. From the shallow, narrow sneaker prints he occasionally found in the sand, he imagined an older woman, small and trim who lived in one of those houses on the west end, and who walked in the morning with her dog. Judging by the prints, it was probably something with size, maybe a shepherd or a retriever. He always left his suit and towel on a bush about a mile away, fair warning for the old gal should she break with habit and take her walk later in the day. Anyway, he would see her coming from a long distance and could take a dip until she moved on.

On most days the sea on this leeward side of the island was like glass, shimmering a bit with the sun and breeze, but at the shore not even lapping. The hungry gulls and industrious little pipers seemed in perpetual motion. But everything else here spoke a warm, soft language of peace, fostering the fanciful notion that if he stored enough of all this before leaving, there would be nothing back home he could not face.

And that thought suddenly prompted unguarded speculation on what in fact might be waiting back there.

A call, perhaps, from Anthony Peoples? What had happened these last few weeks since Peoples had broken it off and said he was leaving town for good? Had time somehow produced enough reassurance to bring him back?

Did he really want to go after his old pal Billy, with everything that would certainly entail? Or would life really be easier if he never heard from Peoples again? Of course there were other journalists in town the guy could go to. How would he feel if somebody else got the story? He knew the answer and felt frustration rise with the realization that there was not a damn thing he could do about it anyway. There was no way he could contact Peoples, other than more pleas on the newscast, and if the fellow was really no longer in town, he would not even hear them.

And what about Sherie? What in the world was he going to do about Sherie after that night they had? "I love you." Those magic words had spilled from his sorry mouth before he had left that evening. Had they been for her or because of Barnes? And what about that little prick, so clearly out to destroy him and with enough column space to do it three times a week? What was he going to do about Barnes? He could be a boy scout for the rest of his life, and Barnes could still produce shit to blow him up.

And then there was Marci. How did he really feel about his wife and what did he really want from her? Why had he felt suddenly so bereft when she had announced the divorce? Hadn't he fantasized often in the past year about leaving his marriage and getting together with Sherie? Maybe the question was, how did Marci really feel about him? And what, if anything, did she really want from him? And if they could figure that one out, was he truly capable of giving it?

Confusion, uncertainty, irreconcilable options everywhere he turned.

He suddenly felt something wet on his knee. Looking down he found a big surprise: a handsome brown lab, head cocked, big moist tongue hanging down, and a friendly, eager look in his eyes.

A sharp whistle got their attention, and both he and the lab looked back up the beach. A young woman with blond hair, a green t-shirt, white shorts and sneakers was standing about a hundred yards away. She made a quick sweep of her right hand, and the dog shook his big head. Then she yelled something that sounded like "Chocolate!" The lab barked once and took off running for his mistress.

She waved casually to Frank, then turned and walked away.

Chapter 61

When the phone began ringing inside, Frank had the key in the front door lock, turning it to secure the house. He hesitated for a second. They were headed for the airport where they needed to return the two cars before boarding the 4 o'clock plane for Miami. Turning the lock back and opening the door, he stepped in and heard the chorus behind him.

"Dad!"

"Frank, we're late!"

"Thirty seconds," he yelled back and lifted the receiver on the fourth ring. "Yes."

"Frank, it's Dennis. I was hoping I'd catch you. I figured..."

"Yeah, Dennis. I was locking the door. What's up?"

"Frank, I got Anthony Peoples on hold. I hope. He sounded pretty skittish, but I got him to agree to let me try to patch him through to you."

"Great, let's try it."

"Okay, if this works, the next thing you hear will be Peoples."

The silence on the line lasted for several seconds. About to say something, he finally heard, "Frank? Hello?"

"Anthony is that you? This is Frank. Can you hear me?"

"Yeah, I hear you."

"Great. So how you doin'? You okay?"

"Yeah, I'm okay. I was thinkin' about comin' back."

"That's great, Anthony. I don't know what they told you, but I'm just returning from vacation today. I'll be back in town tonight. When can we meet? I can even do it tonight if we do it late."

"Naw, I ain't comin' back yet. Not at least until Thursday. I need some time to make sure of some things."

"So okay, where are you? I could even come to you if you think it's safer."

"No, no. I'm comin' back, and I'll lay it all out with the tape and everything. But I gotta do it my way."

"Okay, that's a deal. When will I hear from you again?"

"I'm thinkin' Thursday."

"Okay, that's great. I'll arrange to have a camera ready to do something maybe Friday morning. I want to make sure we do this for you as soon as possible. Because once we go public, you're in a much safer place."

"Yeah, well, maybe. I'll call you."

"I'll be waiting, Anthony."

Chapter 62

With its usual lunch-time business crowd, the Black Knight was bustling, and in the relative privacy of the high-backed Booth One, he sat with his friends O'Bryan and Dworkin. He hadn't spoken to either of them in weeks, but when Peoples had called again this morning saying he was back in town, this lunch meeting had been arranged in no time flat.

Having walked in five minutes early, he had found them deep in discussion with none-other-than Wil Barnes. So intent were they on the little prick's every word that it had taken them a few seconds to notice Frank standing there. Had it all been calculated? Had they wanted him to find them conspiring with Barnes, their swallowed embarrassment all part of the act?

So occupied had he been with such questions that when Barnes promptly retreated from the booth saying, "Hey, Frank, nice tan," all he'd come up with was, "Beat it, you little bitch."

After the usual preliminaries about family and friends, Frank finally asked what they'd been huddled about with Wee Willy. The judge exuded an almost preternatural calm as he drawled, "Frank, Barnes is after us every other day for shit he can use on you. We've been stonewalling him, but we thought you should know what he's doing."

Frank eyed first one earnest pal, then the other. "You guys are just a couple of princes. So how does the murder of Prentis Gant fit into all of this?"

Sam got more interested in his food, but the judge didn't blink. "Into all of what?"

"You know what I'm talking about."

"No, I really don't. But in any case, murder isn't what the the coroner and the prosecutor called it. They said it was suicide."

"Yeah, well, murder's still my theory."

There was silence as Sam chewed his cud, then wiped his mouth with the big white cloth napkin. Finally, he said, "Well, actually, now that you mention it, we were wondering why you'd be paying a midnight call on Prentis Gant. I mean, first you repeat the absurdities of an asshole like Randal Byrd. And then you go calling on a guy who absolutely hated our guts."

Surprised they would admit it, Frank asked innocently, "Why did Gant hate you?"

Dworkin frowned. "He hated me from the day we started in the prosecutor's office together. I guess it was some kind of jealousy thing. And Billy he hated for showing him up in court. The guy was an okay politician, but trying a case, he was a total incompetent."

The judge chimed, "Frank, we're just concerned that people with an axe to grind have been feeding you garbage about us. And because you're under a lot of pressure, both personally and professionally, you might go off half-cocked."

Frank smiled. "People with an axe to grind. You mean like Anthony Peoples? He thinks you murdered his wife and kids."

Dworkin looked up sharply. "What?"

The judge said nothing, shaking his head in apparent amazement as Frank continued. "Oh, he's sure it was a mistake, that the car bomb was intended for him and for the videotape he says he's got showing the two of you taking a payoff."

Dworkin nodded three times, then spoke with the sound of perfect reason. "Frank, this is not believable stuff. You're talking to dope dealers, murderers and professional liars. Surely you don't believe this shit."

Frank gave them another mild smile. "Sam, right now I'm just listening. But what I'm hearing is pretty disgusting, and if it turns out to be true, you can take it to the bank that I'll be breaking the story."

Dworkin turned his corpulent face to the judge. "Un-fucking-believable!"

There were several seconds of silence as Frank leaned back and stared at his two friends, his smile still there.

Finally the judge uttered a sigh and stared back. "Look, buddy, let me make this perfectly clear. What you're saying is tripe. It's garbage. And if you repeat any of it in public, your career as a broadcast journalist will be down the toilet. For openers, you can expect lawsuits for libel and slander that will tie you in knots for the rest of your life."

Dworkin adddded, "And as of this Sunday, we've got Sherie all lined up with Barnes, and she's ready to sing. All we do is say the word."

Frank dropped the smile. "Well, old friends, we all know what truth does to libel laws, so my advice is, go ahead and give Sherie and Barnes the word. Make a pre-emptive strike. Maybe, if it works, you won't have to kill me too."

The counselor and the judge slid their eyes to each other and briefly bowed their heads. The judge said, "Frankie, you're talking absolute nonsense here. I can't believe the words coming out of your mouth."

"Well, I hope I'm wrong, Billy. For once, I really hope I'm wrong."

Chapter 63

At 1:45 in the afternoon in Dr. Ben Stiener's office waiting room there were four women reading magazines, one dabbing at her reddened eyes with tissue and one staring at a wall full of large framed photographs taken by the doctor himself on an African safari. They all looked up with recognition, a couple with mouths open in disbelief, when Frank walked in and headed for the reception window. When he tapped on the glass, Sherie, in nurse's white, looked up with surprised eyes and opened the window.

"Frank, what are you doing here?" Her voice was a whisper.

"I need to talk to you."

Sherie glanced at the gal at a computer nearby and then at the women waiting, everyone of them staring at her. "I'm working, Frank."

"I know. This can't wait."

Sherie again looked around, catching eyes flitting away.

"Sherie, it'll only take a few minutes."

She turned wordlessly to her co-worker, who nodded.

On her feet Sherie opened the door next to the reception window and led him past the waiting room eyes to exit the hallway door. In the corridor there was no one in sight, but, hand on elbow, he walked her several steps further away from the office door. They had not seen each other since their memorable night together almost three weeks ago.

"So what can't wait, Frank?"

Looking down at her lovely scowl, he felt some kind of new presence or authority in her. Maybe it was the antiseptic white, or the way her perfect breasts pressed against the fabric. Whatever, it made him regret even more what he had to say.

"Sherie, I'm sorry it has to be this way. But I can't see you again."

An unnerved surprise covered her lovely face, with a pale quality to those usually vivid blue eyes. "You came here to tell me that?"

"Yes. And a few other things."

"Okay, so talk."

"Look, Sherie, I've always been very fond of you..."

"Fond. That's a nice word. Jesus, Frank."

"Okay, I'm sorry. The thing is, I've been in trouble emotionally over the past year, and you've helped me a lot. I'll always be grateful."

"Hey, don't mention it."

"Look, I know you're angry, and you have every right to be. I know I'm being a cad here, but I'm doing what I have to do. I've got to end this now and try to pull my life together."

"It may be too late."

Feeling close to hopeless, he stared at her. "You're right. I know you've already talked to Barnes or you're planning to, and there's nothing I can do about that. I'd only warn you: steer clear of Sam and the judge. They may be in big trouble themselves."

"Yeah, what kind of trouble?" She leaned back against the wall.

He pulled out an envelope from an inside suit coat pocket. "I can't talk about it now. This is a check for the rest of the lease."

"Ah, the payoff. And the kissoff."

"Call it whatever you want. Just take it. And find yourself someone who's really worthy of you."

Saying nothing and cocking her head slightly, she took the envelope and stared at him. Surprised that his eyes were beginning to tear, he leaned in and kissed her delicately on the mouth. "I'll miss you, darling, in so many ways."

Still leaning against the wall, she simply gazed at him. But her eyes were also getting moist when he turned and walked off.

Chapter 64

Typing furiously at mid-afternoon, working in the pit with Dennis and a half-dozen writers, producers and directors, he stopped occasionally to squint at the screen in front of him but seemed oblivious when Dennis tried to get his attention.

"Frank?"

With no response, the young producer turned in his chair, leaned forward and spoke directly into his right ear. "Frank, you gotta tell me what this commentary's about, or I can't stack this newscast."

Finally, Frank said, "I'm going down to read it to Alice in a few minutes. Don't worry. Just give me two minutes off the top."

The young man shrugged and gave up.

"Okay, you've got it."

Chapter 65

One hour later, high-energy theme music for the five o'clock newscast flooded the control room, and 3-D graphics were bending around the line monitor's screen as Dennis, the director and technicians, all hunched forward in their seats and listened to the urgent, pre-recorded voice of the station announcer: "Here with your news today at five is your award-winning Channel 5 news team: Frank DeFauw and Mary Scott, along with Steve Madden on sports and Mark Adair with the weather.

The director barked, "Take one and...cue him."

In the studio the floor director snapped a finger at Frank.

"Good evening, everybody. I'm Frank DeFauw. Tonight's newscast begins with a commentary that's really kind of a personal confession."

As he continued, his million member audience included Alice Whitney in her office along with Jack Johanson; Jackson and a few patrons in Marvin's Bar; Sherie, still in her white uniform, in her living room; Marci DeFauw along with Jen and Bobby in their family room; Francine and Don Albert in the newsroom; Judge William O'Bryan in his chambers; and Anthony Peoples in a motel room.

"For the past year, ever since the death of my 21-year-old son Tom in a boating accident last summer, I have often indulged in some pretty ugly and unhealthy behavior. I've been drinking too much. I've relied too often on prescription drugs to boost my mood. I've frequently avoided and ignored the people closest to me, particularly my family. I've been less than faithful to my marriage vows. And I've too often shortchanged the good and talented folks I work with here at Channel 5 News, giving less than enough of myself to this job I love so much. In short, I've squandered the trust of everyone important to me, and especially those of you in the viewing audience who expect and deserve nothing less than honesty and integrity from those of us who bring you the news.

"My purpose tonight is simply to ask for your forgiveness. To my beautiful wife Marci, who, of course, has also lived for the past year with the devastating loss of our son: I can only say I'm deeply sorry, darling, for causing you pain. If you can find it in your heart to forgive me, I pledge to do everything in my power to make our marriage live again with love and trust.

"To my daughter Jennie and son Bobby: I love you both more than I can say, and from now on I'll be there for you in a way that I so often failed to be in the past.

"To all of my friends and co-workers: I'll never stop trying to be worthy of the kindness and understanding you've shown me over the years.

"And to all of you out there who turn to Channel 5 for the news you need in this town: my pledge is simply to earn your trust again. That means no more drinking, no more drugs, no more sordid stories about bar brawls and public indiscretions. Just good old-fashioned hard work and dedicated effort to bring you the best, most comprehensive news show possible every single day.

"That's my pledge, folks, and with a little help from the Man Upstairs, we'll make it a reality from this day forward. Mary?"

Sitting next to him on the set, Mary Scott was nearly gaping at him. She turned to one of the studio cameras with a stunned look, then turning back, she put a hand on his. "Thank you, Frank. We're all with you in your battle."

Again she turned back to the camera. "Tonight in our top story, Mayor Coleman Young says he's in full support of his police department's new policy of confiscating the automobiles of those who solicit sex from prostitutes on the streets of our city."

Chapter 66

At the reception desk, Gwen was wearing a phone headset, frenetically busy with the lines. "WTEM." (pause) "Thank you for calling, sir. I'll let him know how you feel." She punched a button. "WTEM." (pause) "Yes, ma'am, I'll pass your words along."

In the VP-GM's office Alice and Johanson faced each other across her desk. His pipe cold in his hand, the news director wondered, "What if he'd come to us with that before the show?"

"Yeah, I was just thinking about that. I'm not sure what I would've done."

"I'm not either."

Picking up her reciever, Alice dialed and waited.

"Gwen, how are the calls?"

At her desk Gwen shook her head. "We're swamped. Maybe 50 so far, and except for a few nasty ones, I'd say all of them positive or supportive in some way."

Chapter 67

In the newsroom with the 5 o'clock just wrapped, Dennis, Francine and Don Albert were sitting together. Dennis seemed to be talking to himself. "'I've been less than faithful to my marriage vows?' Can he get away with that?"

Don said, "If anybody can, it's Frank."

"How about Mary?" Batting his lashes, Dennis did a serviceable imitation of the co-anchor. "'Well, Frank, we're all with you in your battle.'"

Francine had no doubts. "I thought he was wonderful."

"You always think he's wonderful," said Dennis.

Don did his Frank impression: "Good evening, everybody. I'm Frank DeFauw, and tonight I AM the news."

"That's about it," said Dennis. And then Frank walked into the newsroom with a bounce in his step.

"Hey, boys and girls. So far, so good. The calls are running 20 to 1 in my favor."

On his feet Dennis headed for him. "Frank, you were awesome."

Frank shook the young man's hand. "Thank you, my boy, and thanks for your trust. I know I drove you a little crazy."

Don got up as well. "Great work, Frank. Your numbers are gonna go through the roof."

Frank said, "Yeah, well, maybe, probably. Really, I have no idea."

He stopped in front of Francine and did his Bogart. "What'd you think, sweetheart?"

"I thought you were fabulous, Frank. Oh, by the way, Pam in promotion asked me to remind you about that shoot with them tonight at eight."

"Oh, right."

"They said it's just one 30-second spot straight to the camera, so it shouldn't take long."

"Thanks, honey."

As he moved to a computer and searched through some papers, a phone rang, and Francine picked it up. A few seconds later she punched a button and said, "Frank, for you."

He reached for a phone. "This is Frank."

A man's unfamiliar voice said: "A moving little speech, Frank, but you just signed your own death warrant. And maybe one for your family."

He glanced around the newsroom. "Who is this?"

The man on the phone snapped, "Forget that Peoples story, Frank, or you're dead meat." Then he hung up.

Hearing the click, Frank yelled, "Hey, you son-of-a..." and slammed down the phone.

Francine asked, "What's wrong, Frank?"

He picked up his papers. "Just a crank." Up from the chair he headed for his office.

Thirty seconds later the door was closed behind him, as he sat at his desk, as usual piled with tapes, files, newspapers and other debris, and dialed his phone.

After a few seconds: "Hi. So what'd you think?"

"What do you want me to say?" Marci sounded slightly pissed, no different than usual. "Was I moved? Yes. Can I even begin to understand why you chose to say all that on TV? Hardly. I mean, what am I supposed to do, carry a TV set around all day just in case you want to talk to me? Why tell the whole world about our problems?"

He slouched in the chair. "Look, sweetheart, a lot of stuff is happening that I'll tell you about later. Right now, I want you and the kids to get out of town for, a few days. At least until I can break this story. Head up north and visit your folks."

"What story, Frank? What's going on? And why leave town?"

He leaned forward, out of his slouch. "I can't talk about it now, but a guy just called with a death threat, and I want you and the kids out of town."

Still sounding annoyed, she said, "You've had a million death threats, Frank. What's special about this one?"

He got to his feet. "I think I know who's behind this one."

"Who?"

"Billy."

"Frank, you're really losing it."

Chapter 68

The downtown street corner on which he had picked up Letty Pell two months ago was only a block or so from here. As he walked up on the scene, he quickly saw what the promotion folks were after. Bathed in a rare but fading golden light that made even down-at-the-heels Detroit look half-way decent, the location would put the gleaming Ren Cen behind him to serve as both meaningful backdrop and effective backlight for his walk-and-talk.

Had that sticky note from Letty started the slide into his current contemptible fix? No, clearly it was just another garish marker on a long, pathetic descent.

He was only half-listening to the promotion-manager babble of pretty Pam Roberts. "The light is great, and it's pretty quiet down here now, not many cars."

And he was further distracted by the sway of her breasts against her blouse as she swung to gesture down Jefferson Avenue. Jesus, Frank the Incorrigible. So much happening, and he was still pre-occupied with tits.

"And with the camera hidden in the van, we're not as likely to have people trying to get in the shot with you." Pam pointed a toe at a small piece of duct tape on the sidewalk. "This is your starting mark. Now let's move up here where we need you to finish."

They walked a half-dozen yards as Frank stared at the blue van up on the sidewalk a short half-block away and housing the camera to which he'd be playing. As they stepped off the curb into the right lane of the broad divided avenue, a gray Town Car slowed considerably then resumed speed and passed them by.

Pam pointed down at another piece of tape, this one stuck on asphalt about five feet from the curb. "This is the mark we need you to hit. And we need you to come off the curb and into this first lane to get the background we want."

He gave her his this-is-a-piece-of-cake grin. "Gotcha."

148

As he stepped to the end mark and gazed at the van, a hand he knew belonged to Marty, the cameraman, appeared out a window with a thumb's up. With choppy steps in her heels, Pam headed quickly for the van. "Okay, they're happy. I'm going to watch a monitor in the van, so when I wave at you, just start anytime."

"Right, no problem."

Over her shoulder: "I love this light, but it won't last long!"

He walked back to his starting mark, checked his lines one more time from a piece of white paper folded over, then put it away. Pam climbed into the van, and after a moment gave him the wave. He started walking and talking.

"Some people say I own this town. Well, they're wrong. This proud old city belongs to each and every one of you."

In the van Marty worked the camera, James checked Frank's voice on a headset and Pam watched the monitor where Frank's image was well-framed in the attractive cityscape.

"You've lived its history, shared the good times and the bad and cherished a million memories."

The image on the monitor slowly closed in on Frank as he stepped smoothly off the curb and onto the right lane.

"So this city belongs to you. But do I know this town? You bet I do. I was born and raised here, and after twenty-five years of working its streets, meeting its people and telling its stories, yes, I know this town."

He stopped directly on his mark.

"I like to think that's one of the reasons so many of you join us at five and eleven to get your news. Because we know your town."

Holding his pose for a few seconds, he stared straight at the camera in the van's open window. Finally, Pam appeared at the door, holding a stopwatch.

"Fabulous, Frank. Right on the money. But let's do it one more time just as a back-up while the light's still good."

"Sure enough."

"When you're back at your mark, just count to five and do it again."

"Okay, got it."

Inside the van Pam took her seat and watched Frank on the screen walking back toward the middle of the block, looking again at the script. Pam told Marty, "This time let's move in on him a little sooner

149

and a little tighter."

The cameraman nodded. "Right on."

Back on the sidewalk, Frank reached his starting mark, stuffed the script in his coat pocket and turned to face the van. That gray Town Car was moving to a stop on a side street a half-block behind him. As he straightened his tie, the big sedan paused at the intersection. And as he started walking, it turned the corner in his direction.

"Some people say I own this town. Well, they're wrong. This proud old city belongs to each and every one of you."

The Town Car was picking up speed now.

"You've lived its history, shared the good times and the bad and cherished a million memories."

As he moved off the curb and into the street, he heard the Town Car's roar behind him, and glancing back, saw it aiming straight at him.

Hearing the brief squeal of its tires, he dove for the sidewalk, and, as the big car swerved slightly, he barely escaped its path.

Sprawled on the cement, his heart slammed and his breathing turned to gasps. When he turned on an elbow and managed a look, the Town Car had already raced past the van and was rounding a corner.

Jumping out of the van now, Pam was followed by Marty and James, all of them running to Frank.

Marty got there first. "Jesus, Frank, are you okay?

An elbow and a knee both burned, but his heart continued pounding so hard he wasn't sure about the rest. "I guess," he said finally.

Pam seemed close to tears. "Oh, my god, Frank!

"Man, that was close," said James, master of the obvious.

He felt weak and dizzy, but with each taking an arm, Marty and James helped him slowly to his feet. Marty leaned in close and said, "Just take it easy, Frank. Comin' down from that adrenalin, you're gonna feel a little shakey."

Pam looked into his eyes and cried, "Oh, god, Frank, are you okay?"

Swaying slightly, he said, "I'm all right, I think." He slowly flexed his right arm, then felt the hip on which he had landed. "Just a little sore."

As two couples stopped nearby and watched, Marty said, "Christ, was that guy trying to kill you?"

"Yeah, maybe. Or at least scare the hell out of me."

Marty said, "Scared me, man. I saw him comin', but it happened too fast to yell."

Frank glanced at the two couples, one black and one white, and joined now by a bearded black guy who looked like he lived on the street. "Anybody catch the plate?"

They all shook their heads, and Marty said, "It all happened too fast, man."

James brushed off the shoulder of Frank's suit, soiled and bruised. "That was some move, man. You still got the old reflexes."

Frank shook his head without a word.

Chapter 69

More than an hour later, at 9:40 pm, Frank glanced in his rear view mirror at the Bloomfield Hills squad car following the Viper as he weaved through his lakeside neighborhood. When he turned up his drive, the squad car pulled to the side nearby. Parking and walking to his front door, he held up five fingers for Officer Jerry before moving inside.

In the large family room at the back of the house, he strode directly to the huge picture window overlooking the lake and pushed a button to close the drapes. As the motor hummed, he turned to find his wife and son staring at him on the large curved sofa facing a 32-inch Sony that offered "Home Improvement" without sound.

Seriously annoyed, Marci said, "Frank, so why haven't you told the police?"

He glanced at Bobby, who was scowling now. "I *have* told the police. I just stopped at the chief's office and asked for some help. He's only got a few men available tonight, but one of them followed me home, and he's watching the house."

Marci leaned forward on the sofa. "If someone wants to get us here, one little Bloomfield cop won't stop 'em."

"That's why you and the kids need to go up to your parents tonight. You leave soon, you'll be there by midnight."

"Why not the Detroit police? They have so many more people and resources."

"Because Peoples thinks they may be involved in this corruption thing too. At least one or two of them anyway. We can't risk it."

Bobby shook his head. "If we go up to Grandma's, what are you going to do?"

"I'll spend the night at the Airport Ramada. I've arranged to meet Peoples there in the morning. I'll make sure I'm not followed, and the station is sending a couple of security guards to stake out the room, so I'll be fine."

"Rent-a-cops?" Bobby sounded incredulous.

"Don't worry, I'll be fine."

As Marci got to her feet, Frank glanced at Tim Allen on the Sony. He'd met Allen a couple of times at the station on promo tours. Seemed like a nice guy but bottling some kind of strange anger.

"Why are you doing this, Frank?" she asked, "For what? You're risking your life and maybe ours for some guy who was charged with murder. And for a story that won't make any damn difference."

He turned to her. "It makes a difference to me. That's all I can tell you. If I don't do this story, it's like my work means nothing, and my job is a joke."

"What story, Daddy?"

His daughter was standing in the doorway.

"Oh, it's a long one, baby."

Jen moved into the room. "What's going on? Why is there a cop waiting out in front?"

Marci stared at Frank and said, "Someone tried to kill your father tonight."

Bobby also stood and used the remote to turn off the Sony. "Some guy drove by and tried to hit Dad while he was doing a stand up downtown."

"Hit? You mean with a gun?" Jen kept moving, straight for her father. "Daddy, please tell me what's going on?"

He folded her in his arms, grateful for the contact. "Not a gun, with a car. And I don't know if he was really trying to hit me. It may have been more of a scare tactic. The important thing, honey, is that you and Mom and Bobby are spending a night or two up north at Grandma's until this thing is settled."

Jen leaned back and glared at her mother. "What thing? Why don't I know anything about this?"

Marci ignored her. "How's it going to get settled, Frank?"

"Look, if the tape Peoples gives me really incriminates the judge, I'll do the story tomorrow night, and it'll be all over. Once this thing hits air, Peoples will feel safe enough to go to the feds, and the heat'll be off. I'm a target only as long as I'm helping Peoples go public and get to the feds."

Marci walked out of the room with an angry step.

Chapter 70

In darkness now, Bobby got behind the wheel of a white Navigator, Jen was already in the backseat, and Marci was walking out of the house. Carrying a garment bag and a small suitcase, Frank closed the front door and followed her to the back of the big SUV. In the hatch, he placed the suitcase next to a couple of other small bags.

"Marci, I'm sorry about all this. I know it's unfair to you and the kids, but really there's no other way right now."

"Well, we've always taken a backseat to your job. I hope you get your story."

Next to the open front passenger door, he tried to caress her shoulder, but she turned away. He said, "Please believe me, honey. What I said tonight on the show is the god's truth. I love you, and I'm going to make it up to you and the kids."

She turned back to him. "Why did you do that, Frank? Why that whole confession thing on TV?"

Looking into her angry eyes, he wondered how much he should say. "Listen, they were trying to blackmail me. Apparently that little prick Barnes is going to do a big spread this weekend with a lot of dirt. And they were threatening to give him a lot more dirt if I didn't drop the story. So I did the confession to counter all that."

She gazed at him for a second. Were those hazel eyes maybe softening a bit? "You know, Frank, your trouble is, you're so good at delivering a message after all these years of working over your audience, even you don't know whether or not you're telling the truth."

No, her look had not softened, but he thought there might be an opening here. "If anybody knows, darling, it's you."

She glanced at Bobby in the car. Their son was obviously hanging on every word. "No, I'm as clueless as everybody else. I also have no idea why I should, but I still love you, Frank."

He kissed her delicately on the mouth, then gave her a grateful grin.

She said, "Please be careful."

He nodded. "Of course. Just don't worry."

She climbed into the Navigator. "Yes, silly me. What's to worry?"

He leaned down and winked at Bobby. "Take care of your mom."

The boy answered with an obvious effort to stay cool. "Yeah, drive carefully, Dad."

Jen didn't wait for him to turn her way. "We love you, Daddy."

"I love all of you, baby. See you soon."

As the SUV rolled down the drive, he moved to the Viper, dropped the garment bag on the passenger seat and got in. Turning the ignition, he watched his family turn right and drive past Officer Jerry.

A moment later he rolled up next to the patrol car and lowered his window. "Hey, thanks for this, Jerry. Can you make sure they get to I-75 without being followed?"

"Sure thing, Frank. No problem."

Chapter 71

On the road that twisted away from the lake, he came to the 4-way stop where Officer Jerry had been waiting that night three months ago, hidden partially behind that huge elm on the left. When Frank had cruised through the stop, then stepped on it, weaving home after way too much wine with Sherie, Jerry had stopped him two blocks later. Face to inebriated face, the young officer could have put him in a world of trouble that night. Instead, the guy had urged him to negotiate the last few blocks home with care, get himself to bed and sleep it off.

He already owed Officer Jerry big time. And now his help tonight. Maybe a nice box of steaks when all this was over.

The base of the elm was not occupied tonight, but with only a quick glance to his right before taking off again, he missed catching a glimpse of the black Taurus waiting in the darkness up a side road to the left. Its lights off, the Taurus moved promptly to follow Frank.

For a while it kept a considerable distance from the red tail-lights of the Viper rolling through residential streets and heading for Woodward Avenue. But when Frank turned south onto the divided boulevard and merged with the flow of traffic, the Taurus had it easier. And easier still on I-696 east and I-75 south.

Ten minutes later as he moved through heavier city traffic, Frank continued checking his rear-view mirror. Any chance he'd caught a tail? Not likely, but this was no time for guessing.

When he pulled up to the entrance of the Black Knight and spotted his favorite car jockey running toward him, he climbed out and tossed the car keys high in the air. The kid arrived just in time to grab them.

"Hey, Andy, this is your lucky night."

"Whoah! How you doin' Mr. D.?"

"I got a deal for you, Andy. You keep those, and we trade rides until, say, 10 am tomorrow. Deal?"

"Until tomorrow? Deal!"

Rolling slowly into the restaurant's drive, the black Taurus paused for a moment, then continued moving toward the back parking lot as Frank walked with the valet kid into the vestibule. Rolling into a spot near the back end of the lot, the Taurus shut down. A minute later the Viper appeared and nosed into a spot reserved for the valet service. The valet kid got out and ran back to his duties.

One more minute and Frank emerged from the Knight's service entrance and walked quickly into the lot. From the Viper he pulled out the garment bag, then searched the vehicles parked against the back fence. Finding a dirty, 10-year-old Ranger pickup, he opened the door, tossed in the bag and slid behind the wheel. He had to turn the ignition twice before the Ranger's engine kicked in, then he moved toward the lot's back exit.

The Taurus was once again on the move.

Chapter 72

The take-off roar of a 747 actually rattled the window of Room 17 at the Airport Ramada, a long, two-story building with an exterior entrance to each room. At the door to 17, two armed, uniformed security guards sat on straight-backed chairs.

One of them tilted back on two legs, leaning against the motel wall. "What's he doin' with an old pickup? I thought he drove one of them Vipers. Like supposedly they only made 200 of them suckers last year, and he got one."

His partner sat forward, hunched over, forearms on knees, smoking a cigarette. "Who the fuck knows? They say he's fuckin' nuts." He took a long slow drag, then lifted his head and blew. "Anyway, this is gonna be one long-assed night."

"Hey, last time you looked was they payin' you?"

"Yeah, almost enough to buy his gas."

Chapter 73

Inside, 17 was a long, narrow room brightened somewhat with four large prints over the two beds, tracing in abbreviated fashion the history of commercial aviation. Frank was paying them no attention as he sat in his undershorts on one of the beds. He was also ignoring Letterman chatting away with Madonna about where she learned to play baseball for "A League of Their Own."

Instead, he was gazing at a wallet-sized snap shot of his dead son Tom. And then seemingly out of nowhere, an image suddenly popped into his head of Tommy at 21 months, clamped in his car seat in the back of their old Pontiac, watching with those big brown eyes out the window at a brilliant autumn afternoon as they cruised through their old neighborhood in suburban Pleasant Ridge. It was lined with modest homes and all those big red and yellow Oaks and Maples. And filled with the boy's delight, his little voice had announced, "Daddy, the trees are flowers!"

He had known then that his first-born son had the soul of a poet.

And now following immediately was an intensely vivid memory of how he had so often felt at moments like that, with Tommy and, of course, with the other kids as well. A totally desperate and hopeless love that let him know without a doubt that he could not survive the news of something awful happening to one of his children.

In those days, if some random, nightmare thought occurred involving one of the kids, he was simply not able to hold it in his mind. His brain would reel away in terror. He could not bear it. Over the years, as the children had grown older and seemingly a bit less vulnerable, that feeling had abated slightly, or at least occurred a bit less often.

Until that unthinkable August day a year ago when the nightmare had actually happened. And he had, in the end, not fallen apart.

Over the next days, weeks and months he had continued to hold it together, for Marci, Jen and Bobby, for friends too moved or worried to know what to say, and yes, for the tough, unyielding public persona that over the years had actually become part of how he saw himself.

In the end, perhaps, the most powerful motive force had been a fear that never left him, that had simply not allowed thinking or feeling much about his son, that had always threatened to confirm the haunting old certainty that losing a child was something he could not endure.

So many times in the past year he had stopped himself from replaying memories like, "Daddy, the trees are flowers!" Until just the past several days when on the island that locked door had begun to crack open.

Now his first tears since the funeral were running on his cheeks. And he simply let them come.

Chapter 74

The bright mid-morning sun's gleam on the Airport Ramada's once-white walls only revealed their grime. Next to the dirty Ranger pickup in the parking area in front of Room 17 was the blue, unmarked Channel 5 van. And moving into the parking lot now was the red Viper. Rolling slowly until it got close to the pickup, it then wheeled into an adjacent empty spot, roared and shut down.

Out of the roadster popped Andy in jeans and a windbreaker. He looked around, then called to the security guy, who was up out of his chair with a cigarette, "Frank told me to bring it here."

The guy took a drag. "Yeah, he said."

Andy looked back one last time at the Viper, then climbed into his pickup. He leaned down for the keys under the seat and then took three tries at the ignition to get it started.

Chapter 75

The good-sized interior of Room 17 was so jammed with people and equipment that it now seemed only a small, cramped space. In his navy suit and red tie, Frank leaned forward on a straight-back chair, leafing through pages of notes. On a tripod over his right shoulder was a Beta Cam, manned until two minutes ago by Marty, who had announced he had to take a leak.

Two stand lights were shining at a second straight-back chair occupied by Anthony Peoples, his long, narrow hands fidgeting in his lap.

The bulky black audio tech James had clipped a mike to a lapel of the frayed brown sport coat Peoples was wearing over a black t-shirt. Sitting on one of the beds next to his audio equipment, tape boxes and colored lighting gel, James put his headset on and gazed at the portable monitor occupying the other bed with the image of Anthony Peoples on screen. Also on that bed sat the second security guard, hunched over but keeping his eye on the door. Marty finally came back to his camera, gazed into the eyepiece and made sure of his focus.

Frank was still looking at his notes. "How we doin', Marty?"

"Give it five seconds, Frank, and I'll have speed."

Frank glanced up at the security guard. "Luke, for this part I'd like you to sit outside with your partner and keep us safe and sound."

Luke nodded and went to the door. "Okay, Frank."

Once the door closed, Frank picked up a Hi-8 videotape cassette from the bed next to him. "So, Anthony, let's get to how this videotape was made."

Anthony nodded but said nothing.

"First, tell me how this meeting with Judge O'Bryan and your attorney Sam Dworkin was arranged."

"Okay, well, like I said, I told Dworkin I got the fifty grand, all in

162

twenties and such—like he said the judge wanted. But I said I won't do the deal less I can give it to the judge myself. And with him there too."

"You mean Dworkin."

"Right. The judge and Dworkin. Cause I said I need to see the judge take the money and say I'm getting' off. And Dworkin I wanted so I'm not accused by the judge of tryin' to bribe."

"And they agreed to this?"

"Yeah, well, first they said no. No way. I should put the cash in a bag and bring it to Dworkin's office. So I says then no deal. I'll just be takin' my chances and get me a different attorney. Cause I'm innocent of this shit anyway."

Frank's face did a quick grimace. "Again, Anthony, I know this is emotional stuff for you, but if you can avoid using the vulgarisms, we won't have to bleep you and we'll both be better off."

Peoples nodded. "Sorry."

"So anyway, you said no deal, and they changed their mind?"

"Yeah, they changed it, but not right away. Took about two weeks, and Sam kept sayin' the case against me was strong, was gonna put me away for good, never see my family again, all kinda bullshit." Peoples shook his head. "I mean lies."

Frank grinned. "It's okay, Anthony. In the meantime you're talking with the prosecutor, Mr. Gant. And he's telling you what?"

"Well, Gant, he already told me there's no good case on me. And he says, just hold on, their greed is gonna get 'em. They are just too greedy to pass on fifty grand."

"Okay, so tell me something, Anthony. Why did you do this? Why agree to cooperate with Gant?"

Peoples shrugged his shoulders and said nothing.

"I mean you were putting yourself in some jeopardy. And as it turned out, you lost your family over this. So why do it?"

The grooves in his black face getting blacker, Peoples twisted a bit in the chair. "I dunno. Maybe *I* got greedy."

"Greedy?"

"Yeah. Cause Gant said he would get me a job, a good one."

"What kind of job?"

"He said investigator for the prosecutor's office."

"So you did it for the job, to support your family, for the security that a good job would mean."

"Yeah, well, Juanita, my wife had a job. She was workin' at the bank and doin' okay. She was basically supportin' us. And I couldn't find much of nothin' in this town."

Frank looked into the black man's face, those haunted eyes staring at the floor. "So anyway, Anthony, the judge finally agrees. What happened at this meeting?"

Peoples looked up finally and gathered himself. "Well, I go to the courthouse like they said, with this bag fulla cash. Gant said it was all marked and all. And I went to the judge's courtroom and the bailiff, you know, the po-lice that works with the judge there, he put me through the metal detector they got for the courtroom."

"To make sure you're not armed or wired or something. So then what happens?"

"So then he takes me through the courtroom to the judge's office, off the hallway in the back there, behind the courtroom. And we did the deal."

"Okay, before we get to what everybody said, tell me how this was videotaped."

"Yeah, well, Gant, he figured the judge wouldn't want any place but his own chambers, like in his office there. And Gant knew about this janitor's closet off the hall and right next to the judge's office. And in the middle of the night, I guess, they hid this little TV camera in there and cut this little hole in the wall."

"And they were able to get what happened with you and the judge and Dworkin on tape?"

"Yes, sir, that's what they did, just like you saw."

Chapter 76

At the back end of the Ramada lot, the fellow wearing the hooded sweatshirt over a ball cap slouched in the black Taurus. With the seatback lowered so only the top of his hood was visible, he could still look through the steering wheel at the Viper, the unmarked Channel 5 van, and the entrance to Room 17. The electronic buzz of a car phone cut the silence.

"Yeah. (pause) They're still in there. (pause) If they come out together, I could... (pause) Yeah, the rent-a-boys are still here. But anything we do now's gonna be messy. You shoulda let me do him last night. (pause) Okay."

He clicked off the phone, put it down and thought, yeah, very messy indeed. Last night was the time, even with the rent-a-boys there. But he and the judge were not on the same page. Maybe there'd still be a chance to do the newsboy on his way back to the station.

Of course, it was only dumb fucking luck they were in this fix at all. The idiot Peoples was supposed to have his family out of town, and the pea-brained big mouth Byrd should have been at the bottom of the river a long time ago.

Still, he had the exit plan. Just head for his little 21-foot runabout at the marina in St. Clair Shores, buzz across the lake to enter Canada unnoticed by docking at a friend's cottage, and then drive the old clunker he kept there into the wilds of the north woods. With a pile of cash and new ID documents good enough to let him globe trot anywhere he wanted.

But the fact was, with another few years to feed the kitty in the Caymans, he'd then be in a much better position to keep himself comfortable into a pleasant old age. So if there was any chance to keep the current deal working, he had to take it.

Picking up the binoculars, he moved them in a slow scan past the Viper and the van, and just as he got to room 17 and the guards smoking, the door opened and Frank came out carrying the garment bag.

The guards apparently wanted to shake his hand, and Frank obliged. As he walked to the Viper, he looked around, but his gaze slid right past the Taurus.

Chapter 77

Opening the Viper's driver side door, he tossed the bag inside and climbed in. A reach under the seat produced the keys. Backing out of the parking space, he headed for the driveway. By the time he reached the street, the Taurus was moving.

Quickly on his car phone, he traveled a busy surface street leading away from the airport and heading for I-94.

"Fay, I'm 20 minutes away. You won't believe what I've got to show you. (Pause) Yeah, we're gonna blow this old town wide open. (Pause) Look, I didn't want to say anything until I was absolutely sure of it. And I'm not saying anything now, the way these phones broadcast. It'll have to wait 'til I see you. Just tell Dennis I've got a wet dream with Peoples. I'll need at least the first two blocks, maybe three."

He moved the Viper onto the eastbound ramp to I-94, at the moment more focused on this phone conversation than on anything else in his world, and oblivious to the Taurus keeping pace two cars behind.

In the freeway's light traffic both cars were soon moving past the 70 mph speed limit, the Viper sailing down the middle lane.

"No, this story can't wait." (pause) "No, believe me, there are lives at stake here."

For some reason—perhaps the echoing import of what he had just said—he glanced at the right-side mirror and was shocked to find a black sedan racing up so fast, it would be on him in a second or two. Turning back over his right shoulder, he saw the black Taurus pulling even and in its open window, pointing directly at his face, was the barrel of a large black handgun.

"Shit!" he screamed, dropping the phone, ducking and jerking the wheel to the left just as a hooded guy with black wraparounds fired the gun, and the Viper's passenger side window exploded. Tires screeched, a second shot cracked and metal screamed against

167

concrete as the Viper glanced off the median divider. Wrestling with the wheel, he barely managed to keep the car on four wheels as it swerved wildly between lanes and the Taurus was forced to back off.

Finally, pointing the Viper's nose down the freeway, he jammed the accelerator to the floor, and the roadster roared away. For a few seconds, as he glanced in the rear view mirror, the Taurus looked almost as if it were parked.

"Jesus Christ, Fay, are you there?" He glanced at the glass shards in his lap and spotted the phone on the floor in two pieces, the battery dislodged from its impact against the dash.

Within seconds there were vehicles ahead to deal with, two sedans and a pickup in the left and center lanes and a semi in the right. All of them were doing no more than the limit. A look in the mirror showed the black Taurus closing the distance between them, so he swerved to the right, used the paved shoulder to pass the semi, then floored it again as the trucker blared his horn.

"Yeah, I know, buddy."

His heart was still pounding in his chest, but for two minutes he had nearly clear sailing, easily blowing past several cars and trucks, the speedometer pegged past 130. With an exit coming, a glance in the mirror told him that the gunman in the Taurus, though quite a ways back, could still see him leaving. The freeway seemed the better bet.

But where the hell were the cops when you needed them, the blue state police bubbletops or those sneaky black unmarked jobs that were always lurking on the median or behind a bridge abutment? How about a flasher or a siren right now?

No such luck.

What about the phone? As he tried to reach for it, he knew he'd have to slow considerably to grab and put it back together. Forget it.

Another glance at the mirror showed the Taurus just a speck back there, but just as he started to breathe more easily, he sailed around a curve, and, suddenly, not far ahead he was staring at a heart-stopping collection of taillights. Braking hard enough to squeal and lose rubber, he tried to sit tall to gauge the size of the jam. It looked massive.

"Fuck!"

Swinging hard to the right, he flew recklessly up the shoulder past row after row of jammed vehicles, for at least a half-mile. Then ahead he saw others who had tried this same tactic, and their taillights were beginning to flash. With a glance in the mirror he saw several vehicles that were following him up the shoulder. Then stomping on the brake pedal, he got the Viper to a sliding, screeching halt, barely avoiding the rear end of the last in a line of five now stopped on the shoulder by a bridge repair project. Twisting for a look back, he spotted the Taurus also skidding to a stop on the shoulder, maybe six cars back.

Frozen for a second, considering his options, he finally bolted. Running between cars and trucks he looked back to find the guy with the wrap-arounds and black hood climbing out of the Taurus and heading after him. A knife point of panic stabbing at his chest, he raced ahead, trying to run flat out for the first time in how long? His body felt awkward and strange — the muscle memory remained from years ago, but the execution seemed stiff and labored. One more backward glance showed the black-clad guy gaining on him.

"Move!" he screamed at himself, and finally, after more than a minute, his lungs on fire, his running mechanics on the verge of break down, he spotted open freeway ahead of the jam. Cops! Of course, cops would be working to free the jam and ready to help him avoid the intention of the asshole in black.

But after several more strides, there were no flashers, no bubble tops, no cops! Just a few helpful citizens trying to direct the removal of a couple of lightly dented sedans to the shoulder. They had just about made it as he reached the head of the jam, and the impatient drivers in front were already beginning to move.

He headed for the left lane, but it was moving the fastest, and the drivers, intent on escape, hardly looked at him. Fear clutching him, he wheeled and found himself face to face with a bearded fellow in construction garb behind the wheel of an ancient Ford pickup. The guy was grinning at him through an open window, lit up with recognition but cool, as if it was an everyday occurrence to find his favorite local TV anchor stranded in the middle of a busy freeway.

"Hey, Frank, you're my guy!"

"Well, buddy, how about a lift?"

"Really? Sure, man. Hop in."

Frank was already moving around the front of the truck to the passenger door. He yanked it open and hopped in, yelling, "Hit it, pal, there's a guy back there trying to kill me."

He slammed the door, his new best friend floored it, and they squealed away. With a glance back, he saw the hooded asshole running hard but still three cars back, his hand beginning to emerge from under his sweatshirt. Within seconds, it sounded like the old pickup had backfired, but the rear window was shattered and its windshield badly cracked. The two new friends were covered with glass.

"Holy fuckin' christ!" screamed the driver, still jamming the accelerator to the floor. "You weren't kidding!"

"No, I wasn't," said Frank over the speeding truck's weird, throaty roar. Sneaking another look back, he saw the asshole, engulfed in traffic now, stowing the gun under his sweatshirt.

"Don't worry, I'll pay for the windows."

"Christ, Frank, how about a new fuckin' truck!"

Chapter 78

Only a handful of people were in the WTEM newsroom at this hour. Dennis and Francine were eating sandwiches and drinking Cokes. Holding up a Detroit News, she read the headline aloud. "'Frank is...Frank!' Yeah, brilliant. So clever."

Dropping the paper, she picked up the Free Press. "'TV Anchor Tells All. Well, Not Quite.' Barnes is so awful, quoting this woman who's supposed to be his mistress."

Dennis swigged his pop. "Hey, Frank scooped Barnes on his own story. There's nothing he can do to hurt Frank now."

"I guess."

"No really. Frank is huge for people in this town. He's the closest thing they've got to a movie star. Actually, he's more than a movie star. Really, he's on that screen and in their homes for an hour and half every night. That's a lot more than they see any movie star."

Francine nodded. "That's true."

Dennis warmed to his subject with a rap he had yet to try on this pretty, eager young woman. "In some ways he's exactly like them. He's flesh and blood. He grew up here. He has these problems with drinking and women. But, as far as they can see, he always knows precisely what to say and exactly what he thinks. He's never uncertain or confused. He always knows exactly who he is. I'm convinced most people think TV confers some kind of absolute identity. Most of us are never really sure who we are. But Frank is always Frank."

In time to overhear this last line, Frank walked into the newsroom looking exhausted, sweaty and disheveled. But wired with some kind of strange energy, he said, "That certainly sounds profound."

Dennis looked at him. "Frank, what happened to you?"

He kept moving toward his office at the back end of the newsroom. "It's a long story. By the way, did we get my car back here and get some pictures?"

"Yeah, we got it. So what's going on? What's the road rage about? I mean I know you're working the Anthony Peoples thing, but…"

"Yeah, I told you, I'll need at least the first two blocks, right?

Dennis was clearly uncomfortable but knew his anchor was currently unstoppable. "Okay, so what's going on, Frank?"

Frank finally turned back. "I'll tell you in a few minutes. First, I've got to look at something one more time. Anybody seen Fay?"

Francine was hanging on his every word. "I think she's in your office."

"Okay. By the way, Frankie, we're probably gonna need B-roll of Judge William O'Bryan and the defense attorney Sam Dworkin. See if you can dig up some archive stuff."

"I'll get right on it, Frank."

"Good. Oh, a couple of other things, Dennis. We need extra security here today. We need a couple of cops. Detroit cops, not rent-a-cops. At the front gate and a couple more in the building here. Tell them anything you want to get 'em here. We got death threats phoned in, whatever. Just make sure you get them here, like now. And is our erstwhile news director in his office?"

Dennis shook his head. "At lunch outside the building with Alice, and then they've got a meeting at the mayor's office downtown, something about a crime-fighting, keep-your-porch-light-on night in a couple months. They'll be back after three."

Frank smiled for the first time as he headed for his office. "Good. Keep them out of our hair for awhile."

Chapter 79

In his office, Fay was on his cluttered couch reading and marking up interview transcripts. She checked him out. "Well, look what the cat dragged in."

He dropped into his desk chair. "Honey, you can't imagine what this morning's been like."

From a coat pocket he pulled a Beta videocassette. "This is a dub we made this morning of a Hi-8 cassette. It's from a hidden camera. I want you to take a look and tell me what you think. I may be too close to this stuff."

He slid the Beta cassette into a playback machine in a cabinet next to a TV monitor. Flicking a switch and pushing a couple of buttons, he then half-sat on the edge of his desk to watch.

On the TV screen, video snow gave way to a washed out black-and-white picture of Judge William O'Bryan's office in a high-angle shot from one corner. The walls were covered with shelves full of law books. O'Bryan sat behind a large desk with two chairs in front of it. Sam Dworkin was pacing and talking, obviously enjoying himself. The audio was hollow but clear enough.

"So he says, 'What's your take on gun control?' And I say, 'Well, my take on gun control is, guns don't kill people, *shvartzers* kill people."

The judge laughed. "Oh, yeah."

Fay stirred. With mock seriousness she said, "Frank, if you're playing this to embarrass me..."

"Fay, just watch and listen."

On the monitor Dworkin was still laughing in the judge's chambers. "Yeah, the guy about choked."

On screen, there was a knock at the door and Dworkin opened it. "Anthony, my man. Com'on in."

Behind Peoples there was a glimpse of a uniformed cop, but he disappeared as the black man entered holding a canvas bag, and

Dworkin closed the door. "Judge O'Bryan, Anthony Peoples."

Not getting up, the judge stuck out his hand to shake Anthony's. "How you doin', Anthony?"

"Doin' good. How's yourself?"

"Just great. Have a seat."

Peoples and Dworkin sat in the chairs in front of the desk. Peoples held the bag in his lap. Not wasting time, Dworkin asked, "So, Anthony, what's in the bag?"

"What's in the bag is what you said the judge would need to fix my case."

Dworkin: "Well, excellent. Let's have a look."

"Yeah, sure. But, like I said, I need to hear for myself what the judge's gonna do."

"Anthony, I told you what..."

The judge interrupted with a wave. "It's okay. What I'm gonna do, Anthony, is dismiss the armed robbery and murder one charges against you because of insufficient evidence."

Peoples nodded and said nothing. Dworkin twisted in his chair and said finally, "Sounds like a good deal to me."

Peoples stopped nodding. "And if I don't give you what's in this bag?"

The judge cocked his head. "Well, your case is a close call, and I need what's in the bag to convince me you don't deserve to spend the rest of your life behind bars."

Peoples leaned forward and placed the bag on the desk. "Well, fellas, sounds fair to me." He unzipped the bag, turned it upside down and several rubber-banded stacks of bills tumbled into a considerable pile on the desk. "It's all like you said, tens and twenties. Fifty thousand, if you wanna count."

Arranging the stacks neatly on the desk, the judge said, "Oh, I'm sure you counted right, Anthony. In any case, as the old saying goes, we know where you live."

"It's really quite a sight," said Dworkin.

Shaking his head, Frank moved forward and pushed buttons, turning off the tape player and TV set. Then he gazed at Fay. "So?"

The young black woman spoke softly. "You've seen this before, right?

"Yeah, when we dubbed it this morning. Why?"

"I was just wondering if it loses any of its power the second time around."

"Not for me. Judge Billy and I have been pals since high school."

"I'm sorry, Frank."

"I mean, Fay, can this be anything but what it seems? Am I missing something here?"

"I don't think so. We'll need to run it by Fletcher and legal. But I think you got the goods."

Chapter 80

The newsroom was buzzing with the excitement of a major story, with writers, directors, producers and their assistants all intent on various missions. In the pit, his horn-rimmed glasses low on his nose and his shirtsleeves rolled up, Frank was banging away at a keyboard. Next to him, Dennis was on the phone.

"Please let the judge know it's really urgent. We're sure he'll want to respond to our lead story today." Hanging up, Dennis looked at Frank. "They're still saying they don't know where he is."

Frank kept typing. "What about Dworkin?"

"The same."

"Keep trying every fifteen minutes."

"And what about the cops? Shouldn't you be reporting all this to the cops?"

"Not until after we hit air. Peoples says he can't trust anyone, and I've made him a promise."

Chapter 81

At the WTEM front gate, a gleaming black Cadillac with smoked windows had just finished with the gate guard and accelerated up the station's driveway past a parked Detroit Police squad car. Within 30 seconds the Cadillac came a stop in front of the WTEM visitors entrance. Without waiting for the driver to come around to help with the door, out stepped Judge William O'Bryan.

Two minutes later, a secretary ushered Judge O'Bryan into Alice Whitney's office. With Jack Johanson standing to one side, Alice moved with a smile around her desk to shake hands.

"Judge, it's good to see you again."

"Nice to see you, Alice. How've you been?"

"Just fine. Judge, you know our news director, Jack Johanson?"

"I don't think I've had the pleasure."

As the two men shook hands, Johanson said, "How are you, sir?"

Alice gestured to the chairs in front of her desk and moved around to take her own.

"Please make yourself comfortable."

Chapter 82

With Frank still pounding at his keyboard, Dennis asked, "How you comin'?"

"Fine. I'll be done in a few minutes."

"Good. As soon as you've got the narrative, I'll do a chronology and get it up to graphics."

"What do we have for B-roll?"

"There's lots of pictures. Beyond the Peoples interview, we've got the hidden camera stuff, the car bomb, the archive things with the judge and Dworkin. Oh, and that press conference when Gant resigned."

Saying nothing Frank typed: "I first met with Anthony Peoples four weeks ago." He stopped and said, "We've gotta meet with Jack pretty soon."

"He's in with Alice. What about legal? We need Harmon Fletcher's okay."

"Hold off as long as you can. Don't give him time to get nervous and find things we shouldn't say."

From his edit booth across the room from the pit where Frank and Dennis were working, Eddie, in a garish Hawaiian shirt, emerged to call, "Frank, you got a minute?"

Frank didn't look up. "For what, Ed?"

"That stuff from last night."

"I'll be right there."

Eddie returned to his booth, and Frank continued typing. Finally, with one last keystroke, he got to his feet. "Dennis, I just sent it over to you."

"Great."

Frank moved to Eddie's edit booth and stood in the doorway to watch himself on a monitor walking and talking on Jefferson Avenue. "Some people say I own this town. Well, they're wrong."

On the monitor screen he watched the gray Town Car accelerate on the street behind him, moving into the curb-side lane and heading straight for him as he was saying, "This proud old city belongs to each and every one of you...." The Town Car was roaring now as he glanced back, then dove to the sidewalk just in time to avoid being hit. The car quickly squealed out of frame.

Frank moved in closer to the monitor as Eddie stopped the tape and then reversed it. He glanced at Frank. "You screwin' this guy's wife?"

"Yeah, you think he was trying to hit me?"

Eddie looked back at the screen and worked the controls. "Well, at the last second he was actually swerving away, but you can see how close it was."

On the monitor the picture moved forward again, this time in slow-motion. Again the car headed for Frank, and again with little to spare he dove away as it swung past him.

"Pretty close. Ed, can we get a look at the guy behind the wheel?"

"Yeah, I'm working on that."

With both of them riveted to the monitor, Eddie slo-moed the tape up to the point where the car was closest to the camera. Then he froze the picture. The big sedan filled the screen. The driver's face was shadowed and out of focus, and his head seemed to be in a hood.

Frank looked even closer. "Christ, that might have been the guy who was chasing and shooting at me this morning. He was also wearing a hood."

Eddie said, "I don't know if it'll help, but I can use the Quantel to get closer."

Carrying a half-dozen cassettes, Francine stopped in the doorway and looked at the monitor. "This the guy who nearly hit you?"

Without looking away from the monitor Frank said, "Yeah, and maybe shot at me today. You ID him, you're my new co-anchor."

"Hey, good deal! But Eddie, you gotta blow him up and give me a better chance."

"Already doin' it, babe."

Then she remembered. "Oh, Frank, Alice and Jack need to see you right away in her office."

"Yeah, I need to see them too."

Francine moved into the edit room, and Frank walked back to tell Dennis, "Hey, I've got to see Alice and Jack and get them up to speed. Where's the hidden camera stuff?"

"Here you go." Dennis handed him the cassette, and Frank headed out of the newsroom.

Chapter 83

In the VP-GM's office Frank occupied a third chair placed next to Alice's desk. Staring at Johanson and the judge, he felt tense and uncomfortable as Alice spoke with a seriousness he had not heard from her before. "Frank, the judge is suggesting you're out of control. And on the basis of your behavior yesterday and over the past several weeks, I'd have to agree."

"Alice..."

"No, let me finish. Yesterday, without clearing it with either Jack or me, you used your commentary as a kind of self-serving confessional, airing your own personal problems in a way that was just totally inappropriate. And today, again without checking with us, you're apparently planning to run with a story that's likely to ruin two careers—and all of it based on hearsay from a fellow charged with armed robbery and murder. And, I should add, with close ties to a top drug dealer. The judge tells me he has a lawyer working right now to get an injunction against our running the story. But even without that, we've got to pull you off until you can get yourself and your life back under control."

He pulled in a deep breath. "Look, first, that commentary was simply an effort to counter all the shit my old friend the judge here has fed Mr. Barnes lately to fuck up my career. Because he knows damn well the story I've got is not based on hearsay.

"Anthony Peoples was working with the late Prentis Gant to make a bribery case against the judge and Sam Dworkin. And the car bomb that killed Peoples's wife and kids back in May was intended for Peoples and the videotape they knew he had of a certain conversation in the judge's chambers. I've got a copy of that tape right here."

Frank raised the cassette he'd been holding, and the judge finally stirred in his chair. "Frank, you're making a terrible mistake. Alice, I told you..."

Alice intervened. "Frank, the judge told us you might have a tape that only he could explain."

"Fine. Let's play the tape, and then we'll hear what he has to say."

Chapter 84

Back in the edit booth, Eddie was in the process of magnifying the image of the front of the Town Car until just the windshield filled the monitor screen. The picture was grainy and unfocused, but Francine thought she could see something interesting now about the hooded driver's face.

"Sorry," said Eddie, "that's probably as good as it gets."

Francine picked out one of the cassettes she was holding. "Okay, but now, Eddie, can you put this tape in and get it on the other monitor?"

Eddie took the cassette and slipped it into the tape machine. "Anything for you, babe."

Chapter 85

Alice sat with her hands folded on her desk. Along with all three men turned in their chairs, she was watching one of the monitors built into the wall opposite the desk. A stoic look covered each of those male faces, including the judge's, as he watched himself in fuzzy shades of gray on the hidden-camera tape:

"That's. okay, Sam. What I'm gonna do, Anthony, is dismiss the armed robbery and murder one charges against you because of insufficient evidence."

Dworkin: "Sounds like a good deal to me."

Peoples: "And if I don't give you this bag?"

Judge O'Bryan: "Well, your case is a close call, and I need what's in the bag to convince me you don't deserve to spend the rest of your life behind bars."

Peoples: "Well, fellas, sounds fair to me. (pause) It's all like you said, tens and twenties. Fifty thousand if you wanna count."

Judge O'Bryan: "Oh, I'm sure you counted right, Anthony. In any case, as the old saying goes, we know where you live."

Dworkin: "It's really quite a sight."

Chapter 86

Francine and Eddie sat forward in their chairs, still working together in the edit booth. The young redhead liked what she was seeing on the monitor.

"Fabulous, Eddie. How long will it take?"

"To get this on a tape for you?"

"Yes."

"Oh, maybe a whole hot minute."

"Great. I'll make some calls."

"Okay, babe."

Chapter 87

Picking up the remote, Alice got up and moved a few steps around her desk until she was standing next to Johanson and could get a better look at the monitor's picture of the judge's desk loaded with cash.

Frank turned back in his chair. "That's probably enough for now."

Alice pushed a button on the remote, and the monitor went black. She returned to her chair, as Johanson and the judge turned back in their chairs.

Frank gazed at his old friend. "Well, Billy, you want to explain that to us?"

The judge smiled and straightened a bit. Then playing to Alice and Johanson, and almost completely ignoring Frank, he said, "You bet. First of all, the reason I have an attorney filing for an injunction is because that tape belongs to the Wayne County prosecutor's office, and..."

Frank shouted, "Oh, come off it. You know damn well that's prior restraint, and no court is going to give it to you."

The judge finally looked at Frank. "Not so. Not with an on-going investigation involved here."

Frank raised his brow. "An on-going investigation? What the hell are you talking about?"

O'Bryan darted a quick grin at Alice. "If you'll just calm down and listen, Frank, I'll tell you."

Frank shrugged and gestured that the judge had the floor.

With a nod in Frank's direction, O'Bryan continued: "This tape was made because I was working with the Wayne County Prosecutor at that time, Prentis Gant. We arranged to have a hidden camera tape this whole transaction, in an effort to nail Anthony Peoples for attempted bribery."

Frank exploded. "That's bullshit. A judge in cahoots with the prosecutor to get some guy for bribery when he's already up for armed robbery and murder?"

"Anthony Peoples wasn't the main target in all this. It was his cousin 'Pretty Rick' Mahone. We figured Peoples would get the money from his cousin. We could trace the cash back to 'Pretty Rick' and put one of this town's leading drug lords away for a good long time."

Frank shook his head. "Billy, I can always tell when you're bullshitting, and right now, it's coming out of your ears."

Alice got up from her desk again and stood behind it. "Frank, I'll take it from here. From what I've seen and heard, I think it would be wise not to go ahead with this story, at least for the time being."

Frank also got up from his chair. "Oh, for Christ sake, Alice..."

Alice raised her hand. "Frank, that's enough. Jack, what do you think?"

Already knowing what was coming, Frank was shaking his head.

"I agree, Alice. I sure don't like prior restraint. But in this case, I think we need to move very carefully."

Chapter 88

In the station's lobby at the visitor's entrance, Gwen was sitting at her desk and listening on her headset to an irate viewer as she watched Francine running toward her down a long hallway. The young woman was clutching a cassette, and as she reached the lobby she stopped dead in her tracks when she saw the uniformed Detroit Police officer sitting in the armchair watching TV, a large strawberry birthmark covering almost half his face.

Francine stared hard at the man, then glanced at the other two Detroit cops on the couch and finally at Gwen on the phone behind the desk. She turned and walked quickly down an adjacent hall leading toward the VP-GM's office.

Chapter 89

In that office Judge O'Bryan was saying, "Frank, you're just dead wrong on this one."

"Yeah, well, twice in the past two days I've nearly been just plain dead..."

There was a sharp knock on the door, it opened and Alice's secretary Margaret leaned in. "Frank, Francine from the newsroom says she needs to see you right away."

"Maggie, I'm a little busy at the moment."

In the doorway Francine looked over the secretary's shoulder, nodding frantically. "It's like really urgent, Frank."

Reluctantly he headed for the door. "Sorry, I'll just be a minute."

Walking out of the office, he left the door open so he could glance back in as he talked with Francine.

Judge O'Bryan took advantage of the moment. "Alice, I really appreciate the opportunity to come in and tell you about my concerns."

Alice smiled. "I'm glad you called. We appreciate the heads up."

"You know, Frank and I go way back together, and I have tremendous respect for him. But the guy has just put himself under too much pressure lately. He really needs some time off."

Alice nodded in agreement and watched as Frank took the cassette from Francine and moved back into the office. He closed the door and remained standing.

"Look, Alice, just give me two more minutes to explain the rest of this, and then do what you want."

Alice stared at him for a moment, then said, "Two minutes, Frank."

Chapter 90

Moving slowly up the hall, Francine reached the lobby and peered around the corner. The cop with the birthmark was no longer sitting there. She walked quickly to the desk. "Gwen, why was that police officer here?"

"Which police officer?" Gwen glanced at the two uniformed cops on the couch.

"Not those two. The one who was sitting in that chair."

"Oh, he came with the judge who's meeting with Alice."

"Where'd he go?"

"The police officer? He asked if he could look around the station."

"And you let him?"

"Francine, he's the police."

Chapter 91

Holding the floor, Frank felt good on his feet. "The fact is that everybody in a position to incriminate the judge here and Sam Dworkin is either conveniently dead or supposed to be."

Alice nearly rolled her eyes. "What on earth are you saying, Frank?"

"I'm saying that 'Pretty Rick' is dead, murdered in his Maserati. Anthony Peoples is supposed to be dead, by the car bomb that took his wife and kids instead. Prentis Gant is dead, by his own hand, according to the cops, but I saw him that night, and my guess is he was murdered. And finally, I'm supposed to be dead. At least once and maybe twice in the last 24 hours someone's tried to kill me."

Alice's eyes narrowed. "Frank, what are you saying? All I know about is last night, and I was told it was an accident, or a near-accident, that you shouldn't have been walking in the street."

Frank moved to a tape machine on a shelf next to the monitor and ejected the cassette that was in it. "Yeah, well, I'll show you last night, and you can judge for yourself."

Removing a sticky note from the cassette Francine had brought, he slotted the tape into the machine and pushed a button. "But today coming back here after interviewing Peoples, I was chased on the freeway and shot at. I'm lucky to be alive."

"Shot at, Frank?"

"Yeah, Alice, shot at. I had to ditch my car on the freeway with shattered windows and bullet holes in it. We've got pictures of it."

Everyone turned to watch the monitor. On screen Frank was standing on Jefferson Avenue waiting to walk and talk, nicely lit and framed.

"This is what happened last night."

On the monitor, Frank once again started his walk and, as the gray Town Car began turning the corner behind him, spoke his opening lines. "Some people say I own this town. Well, they're wrong. This proud old city belongs to each and every one of you..."

Again, the Town Car accelerated toward Frank. And again it nearly hit him and then continued past until the action stopped in a freeze-frame.

Alice said quietly, "Frank, you were very fortunate."

"Yeah, maybe I was."

Now on the screen the freeze was followed by a magnified version of the frame that produced a fuzzy close-up of the driver's face.

"And we were lucky our camera was more or less hidden and perfectly positioned to get this guy's mug on tape. Remember this face with a big mark there on the left side. I think we're going to see it again."

On the monitor the magnified freeze gave way to a courtroom scene featuring Judge O'Bryan. On screen he was saying, "This court feels strongly that..."

Whereupon the defendant, lunging past the court reporter, went for the judge's throat. "You (bleep). I'll rip your (bleep) head off."

As the bailiff quickly wrestled the man away from the judge, the action again froze, and the picture was blown up to offer a detailed look at the bailiff's face. Now there was a clear look at a large, strawberry-colored birthmark on his left cheek and forehead.

Frank read from the sticky note. "The man coming to the judge's aid, the man with the large red birthmark, is the judge's bailiff, Officer Kenneth Miles. Officer Miles has been assigned to Judge O'Bryan's courtroom for the past three years. And for two years before that, he was a member of the Detroit Police Department's gang squad.

"Oh, and before that he was with the bomb squad."

Now the monitor's screen was split, filled with the two freeze-frame close-ups of the driver and the bailiff. They appeared to be one and the same man.

Frank continued: "And in case you still have any doubts, I'd say these side-by-side pictures strongly suggest that Officer Miles is also the man who apparently tried to run me down last night."

He pushed the pause button on the tape player to keep the split picture on the screen. Then turning back to his attentive audience, he found his old pal the judge finally looking a bit uncomfortable.

"Alice, all I'm saying is, under the circumstances it seems right and appropriate to tell Anthony Peoples's story and to include portions of the hidden camera tape that Peoples gave me. By the way, your honor, if you were really working with the prosecutor to nail Peoples and 'Pretty Rick' for bribery, why would Peoples have the tape in his possession?"

The judge was getting a little pink in the face. "How should I know? This is a guy charged with robbery and murder. Maybe he stole the tape."

"Charges, which you dropped in exchange for a $50,000 bribe."

"That's nonsense."

Frank turned to his news director. "Look, Jack, I'll include the judge's denial and his trumped up tale, if he really wants to stick with it. But this story needs to be told, and we've got everything we need to tell it properly. After which Peoples turns himself into the feds, we give them everything we've got as well, and it's all settled in court."

With a long drag on his pipe, Johanson blew smoke and nodded. "Alice, I think Frank's right."

She stared at Frank for a second. "There's not much time. You better get back to the newsroom."

"Thanks, Alice. I'm sorry, Billy, I really am. If you want to come with me now, we'll put you on camera, and you can have your say."

"Fuck you, Frank. I'll see you all in court."

Chapter 92

Looking desperate, Dennis stood in front of his computer. "Where the hell is Frank?"

As if on cue, the anchorman walked into the busy newsroom.

"So how we doing, Denny?"

"Frank, I was getting worried. We're doing fine, but we've got less than 40 minutes, and I haven't been able to get any response from Dworkin or the prosecutor's office. Francine tells me you and the judge were in there with Alice and Jack."

"Yeah, don't worry about a response. I've got one from O'Bryan."

"Great. I'll insert that while you go over the lead. So what did he say?"

Frank stopped on his way to the back of the newsroom and the hallway to the men's room. "His honor claims he was working with Gant to nail Peoples for bribery."

"What? That doesn't make any sense."

"Of course, it doesn't. But give me a minute here to take a leak and put on my face, and I'll give you a verbatim from the judge. Now what about legal?"

Dennis sat at his computer. "Harmon'll be here in a few minutes, but he shouldn't have a problem. We've been very careful. Everybody has their say, we're just reporting the facts and I've pasted "allegedly" on everything."

"Okay, good." Frank resumed his walk to the back of the newsroom and then through the hallway to the men's room door.

Inside, the place was empty, except for one stall with its door closed. He walked up to a urinal and unzipped his fly.

Chapter 93

Inside that one closed stall, sitting fully clothed in his police uniform, was Officer Kenneth Miles.

He had found this men's room by chatting up a bored stage hand, feigning an avid interest in Frank, and getting the guy to talk about the anchor's pre-newscast routine. After taking a brief look around in here, he had then hung out in a corner of the newsroom, mostly hidden behind a newspaper, until Frank walked in, and it was soon obvious that the full story was a go.

Moving quickly, he had taken an alternate route to get into this stall before the asshole came in whistling to take a piss.

Now through a half-inch space along one edge of the stall's wall, he could see the jerk, with a paper towel in his collar, primping at the mirror. For a second he touched the department-issued .44 in its holster. Then he lifted his right pant leg to grab from its holster the little Walther .22 he had taken off a punk-assed hit-kid with a drug crew a few years back.

He pulled up the other pant leg to expose the gun's custom made silencer strapped to the side of his shin. Then reaching back, he flushed the toilet, and while the noise filled the room, he screwed the silencer into place on the Walther's barrel.

One last thought now on making this little move. The judge was usually a pretty sharp guy, but in this case he'd become rattled and wasn't really thinking straight. With Frank pounding away at it, this story about setting up Peoples and "Pretty Rick" for bribery, even with someone inside the prosecutor's office ready to vouch for it, had little chance of sticking.

No, to give it at least a chance, he needed to put a couple in Frank's head, drag him into this stall, pull his pants down and prop him on the shitter. Figuring he was taking a huge dump, they wouldn't find him for several minutes, and by then he'd be out that back door off the newsroom, to pick up the judge and drive calmly out the station's gate.

Then he'd see how things went and, only if necessary, execute his carefully formulated exit plan.

One more glance through the crack at Frank still primping, and he got up off the toilet, unlatched the door and stepped out of the stall.

Chapter 94

In the mirror Frank immediately saw Miles come out with the gun pointed at him, and he froze, half his face covered with liquid make-up. Only Frank's eyes moved as he followed the cop circling a few steps behind him with the gun held in both hands and leveled at the middle of his back.

In front of the men's room door, Miles stopped moving and asked, "You think that stuff might work for me?"

Frank continued to stare at him in the mirror. Fear filled his throat, but he swallowed hard and tried to keep his voice steady.

"I doubt it. Even with make-up, you'd still look like a killer."

"Say goodnight, Frank. That was your last commentary."

Miles raised his aim to the back of Frank's head and began to squeeze the trigger.

And just then the door behind him swept inward, as the two cops from the lobby burst into the room followed by Francine. The swinging door caught Miles in the back and shoulder as the muffled gun fired with a thud. The bullet hit Frank's mirrored image squarely in the face, shattering the mirror and showering Frank with fragments.

The two cops quickly wrestled Miles to the floor and disarmed him, while Francine rushed to Frank.

"My god, Frank, are you okay?"

Deeply shaken, he tried to breathe and nodded silently as he stared at the slivers of mirror on his suit coat.

After a few seconds he finally found his voice. "Seven years bad luck, Frankie."

The young redhead took his arm and moved him toward the door. "Not for you, Frank. For him. Probably a lot more than seven."

Chapter 95

On the news set, his make-up and hair in place, he felt close to calm as he waited for his cue. The floor director counted down, then whipped a finger at Frank.

"In my twenty-five years in the news business this may be the most painful and perhaps important story I've ever reported. As some of you may know, Detroit Recorder's Court Judge William J. O'Bryan is a long-time friend of mine. But tonight Judge O'Bryan is at the center of a number of serious allegations involving corruption and murder.

"Good evening, everybody, I'm Frank DeFauw. And tonight Channel 5 News has learned exclusively that Judge William O'Bryan, along with prominent defense attorney Samuel Dworkin and at least one other man who works in Recorder's Court, may be involved in an alleged bribery scheme — a scheme that may have led to murder in an effort to cover up their alleged criminal activities."

Chapter 96

Thirty-five minutes later, Frank was finishing his summary of "what we've learned so far," as Channel 5 wrapped its extended coverage of the court bribery expose, which had even included Mary Scott interviewing her co-anchor on the I-94 shooting.

With b-roll running of a chaotic scene in the newsroom, Frank read:

"And just about 40 minutes ago, right here in our Channel 5 studios, in the men's room off our newsroom, a third attempt was made on my life by this man, Kenneth Miles, a Detroit Police officer assigned to Recorder's Court as a bailiff for Judge O'Bryan.

"As you heard earlier, only because of excellent police work by Detroit Police officers Frank Riley and Eric Fontana did I come out of this unscathed.

"Here you see Miles in the custody of Officers Riley and Fontana as they took him away to the Wayne County Jail where he'll be held for an arraignment tomorrow morning in the very court where he has served as a bailiff for the past three years."

Chapter 97

Of course, at 11 that evening, WTEM presented a full report on the alleged bribery and murder scandal featuring Judge William O'Bryan and defense attorney Sam Dworkin and involving Channel 5's own Frank DeFauw as a major player. Again the report included most of what was seen on the five o'clock, but there were significant additions as well.

Anthony Peoples was interviewed by Frank live on the set, talking at some length about the experience of concealing his identity and finding safe refuge for several weeks, both in the city of Detroit, where he was known to a number of people, and in Cleveland, where he knew only his sister Vanessa, and where he had spent nearly four weeks after being deeply shaken by the death of Prentice Gant.

Also interviewed, live from his living room, was the Wayne County prosecutor Peter Canzoneri, who offered absolute assurances that "every step will be taken to get to the bottom of every single allegation" and that "no stone will be left unturned to insure that those who may have broken the public trust are brought to justice."

Chapter 98

Though it would not be seen today, the sun had been up for a while on this frigid February morning, everything in browns, blacks and grays, from the ice covering the lake, to the stripped bushes and naked trees, to the thick cloud banks blocking every inch of sky. Staring at this bleak scene through the kitchen window, he had to admit he was feeling pretty damn good.

Empty nesters now, with Bobby in his freshman year at U. of M. along with Jen, he and Marci seemed to be making the transition okay. Yes, it would be nice to hear more often from the kids, but Marci's more relaxed attitude now was no news was good news.

Her voice came from behind him as she entered the kitchen. "You couldn't sleep?"

He turned to her, the blond hair sleep-tousled, a little crazy, the way he liked it in the morning. "Yeah, no, I had one of those stupid, annoying dreams where nothing makes sense when you wake up, and every time you try closing your eyes, it starts again. You ever get those?"

"No. But I think you just couldn't wait to read the Freep."

They both glanced at the table covered with sections of the paper.

"Well, that might also be true."

She let him kiss her, a soft peck on soft lips, then went for the pot of coffee he had made more than an hour ago.

Half the Free Press had seemed to be devoted to coverage of the trial's conclusion yesterday. Even Wee Willy's gossip column was almost straight reporting on the jury's surprisingly quick return of the verdicts.

Frank rarely looked at the little prick's column these days. Actually, Barnes had pretty much left him alone ever since that strong backlash to the piece on Frank's peccadilloes with Sherie Sloan. Word was the guy had nearly lost his column over that, when even some of his most avid gossip fans had deemed the story both salacious and unfair.

Three months later when the lease on her apartment was up, Sherie had called to tell him she was moving to Pittsburgh for a new job and a new life. He had wished her luck and resisted the urge to see her gorgeous face one last time.

Chapter 99

Upon first sitting at the table that morning with his coffee and the paper, he had quickly discovered the Free Press had pulled out all the stops, assigning extraordinary resources to report the story and developing several background pieces, all poised to grab and illuminate the moment.

According to the paper, the bribery, corruption and murder cases against William O'Bryan and Sam Dworkin had turned on the testimony of two men: the aggrieved widower Anthony Peoples and the judge's bailiff, Detroit Police officer Kenneth Miles.

On the corruption charge, Peoples, bolstered by the videotape that had caused such a sensation when it was first shown on the news, had sunk both the judge and the attorney popularly known as "Suspenders." Despite a variety of detailed and inventive arguments, including the claim of a broken chain of evidence, their high-powered legal team had finally failed to get the tape tossed, and the defendants went down "like a hot knife through butter," as Frank's favorite columnist put it.

The murder charges were more of a contest. Miles, the cop assigned as a bailiff for Judge O'Bryan, had pled guilty to one count of attempted murder in the men's room shooting at WTEM, and one count of reckless endangerment in the Jefferson Avenue incident, both of them involving popular Channel 5 news anchor Frank DeFauw. But after several lengthy and grueling interrogation sessions, Miles had continued to maintain that he had absolutely nothing to do with the bombing deaths of Peoples' wife and two children.

And according to an unnamed source in the federal prosecutor's office, despite his two pleas, Miles had actually claimed that he had never intended to kill anyone. In plea bargain negotiations, Morgan Flannigan, the attorney for Miles, said the tape of the Jefferson Avenue drive-by near-miss clearly showed an attempt to scare, not harm. And in the men's room shooting, Flannigan maintained the only reason the gun had fired was that the swinging door had slammed his client in the back.

In the end, the key to the prosecution finally making a plea deal was a firm avowal by Miles that he had a contract from the judge and "Suspenders" to murder both Peoples and DeFauw. Even with his pleas accepted, Miles would likely be spending the better part of 15 years behind bars.

At trial Miles had been grilled unmercifully for several days on his history, character, motives and contradictions. He held up sufficiently to give the jury enough for a second degree murder conviction for both Dworkin and the judge. They were each headed for 18-25 (12 if they behaved themselves) at some federal pen.

There were two other questions about this story that had continued to intrigue Detroiters, and the paper had diligently searched for answers. One involved the early retirement and subsequent suicide of the Wayne County prosecutor Prentis Gant. The other was how Sam Dworkin and Judge O'Bryan had learned of the existence of that infamous tape.

According to one extensive background report, federal investigators, with information from Anthony Peoples, had looked into the possibility that someone in the county prosecutor's office had tipped one of the men to what Gant was up to. Investigators determined that Gant had run the operation entirely on his own, apparently not trusting anyone in his office. He had personally gone to a federal judge for a warrant, hired a private company to place the camera and secured the bribe money by accessing a cash account normally used to pay informants. When he met with Peoples, it was always alone at a private location.

Then-assistant prosecutor Peter Canzoneri, who had been assigned to the case in which Peoples was charged with a felony murder, had said he had "no clue what Gant was doing." He was also quoted as saying, "I didn't think much of the case, but Gant insisted on going forward with it."

One member of the county prosecutor's staff, who wished to remain anonymous, had said while others in the office could have gotten wind of Gant's operation, Canzoneri was "in the best position to sniff it out and might have had a motive" to pass a word along. According to the source, it was common knowledge in the office that

Canzoneri had long coveted the top job and was bitter about his inability to raise the political and financial backing he needed to make a run for it.

Canzoneri had hotly denied all of this, and federal authorities, unable to come up with anything solid, said they simply had no evidence of any wrong doing in the Wayne County Prosecutor's office.

As for the question of why Prentis Gant had retired after a little over a year on the job, investigators, again with information from Peoples, looked into the possibility that Gant had been blackmailed because his wife reportedly had several relatives in the country illegally, with some of them involved in unlawful activities. The newspaper reported that several of Delores Gant's relatives, including a brother, sister and two cousins — reputedly all illegal aliens — had in fact spent time in the city over the past decade, though often moving back for periods of time to their hometown on the Mexican border. At least twice over the years family members had been picked up in the city, once for marijuana possession and once for dealing in cheap Mexican knock-offs of high-priced prescription drugs, though both times charges had eventually been dropped.

With Gant's resignation most of his wife's clan had scattered and left the city. With Gant's death, Delores, who had become a U.S. citizen when she married Gant back in 1981, put the family home up for sale and moved with her children to California. When contacted there by federal authorities, she had denied that any of her relatives had ever been in the county illegally and said that she had no evidence that her husband had died by anyone's hand but his own.

As for the car bombing, it had to this point gone unsolved. Of course, there had been strong suspicions that it had been directly connected with the bribery case, and Kenneth Miles' history with the Department's bomb squad had certainly pointed a finger at him. But an exhaustive canvassing of that westside neighborhood had failed to turn up a single witness who had seen anyone in the vicinity of the car parked in front of the Peoples' home prior to the explosion. And no evidence of any kind had been uncovered that would even begin to make a case against any of the principals in the case.

Predictably, defense attorneys had managed to float at least one report that Anthony Peoples had been secretly connected with a drug operation competing with his cousin "Pretty Rick," and that the bomb had simply been pay back.

Along with a photo of Anthony snapped by a Free Press photographer on one of his several days of testimony during the trial, the paper had included a brief and, to Frank, less-than-satisfying interview with the man whose family's tragedy was at the center of the story.

"Contacted at his sister Vanessa's home in Cleveland late yesterday, after the verdicts were announced, Mr. Peoples said he was 'satisfied' with the trial's outcome. Asked if he thought justice had been served, he said simply, 'No.' After a pause, he added, 'Not for my Nita and my babies.'

"Later Mr. Peoples went on to say that he would not be returning to Detroit. 'There is nothing for me there now,' he said, 'except bad memories.'"

Chapter 100

At his desk a month later, going through a stack of mail, Frank opened a note from his New York agent. As he expected, it offered news of another rejection of *Buffalos in the City*.

He had started this process with some reasonable facsimile of hope. The agent had said some nice things about the manuscript and thought she could place it. By now every time he saw her distinctive pink stationery, the first thing he thought of was yet another reject. Maybe it was time to try it himself with the Wayne State University Press editor he'd met in that Cass Corridor bar.

A discreet rap on his door was followed by the usual pause. He knew who was out there.

"Enter."

Francine stuck her pretty red head in the office. "Anything I can do for you, boss?" With Fay on a well-earned Florida vacation, she was filling in for the week.

"Ah, the remarkable young woman who saved my sorry, hopeless, degenerate life."

"Frank, would you please, please stop saying that!"

"Why? It's true."

"It's embarrassing."

"So you admit it's true."

"What part?"

They both seemed to love this stupid little game they had been playing off and on for months. He said, "The 'sorry, hopeless, degenerate' part."

"Yes, that part is true."

"Frankie, I've got nothing for you. Go find some real work."

She gave him her light-up-the-world smile and left. And then all those vibrant curls got him thinking about redheads. Letty Pell had called the other day.

"Just wanted to say I miss you."

"Well, Letty, I seriously doubt that, but I've wondered for a long time if my old friend Billy, now of the Lewisburg Federal Pen, really put you up to coming on to me. How about telling me the truth?"

"The truth, Frank? The truth is I've always found you enormously attractive."

"That isn't what I was asking, Ms. Pell, but let's just leave it at that."

Would he call Letty?

Unlikely.

Even he could learn a lesson occasionally.

###

From T.V. LoCicero:

Word-of-mouth

It's vital to any author. If you enjoyed this book, please consider leaving a review at Amazon. It may be only a line or two, but it could make a big difference and would be deeply appreciated.

Be the First to Learn of a New Release

If you'd like to receive an auto email when the next book is released, please sign up at: http://eepurl.com/z26Vv

Your email address will never be shared, and you can unsubscribe at any time.

Say Hello

My website (http//www.tvlocicero) offers info, thoughts, photos, videos and much more. I'd love it if you come by and say hello. You can also get in touch on Facebook, or send me an email: tvloc1@netscape.net

An excerpt from
Book 2 of The *detroit im dyin* Trilogy

ADMISSION OF GUILT

By T. V. LoCicero

TLC *Media*

Chapter 1

New spring leaves, already withering, scratched and whispered in the few Dutch Elms still standing on this dark, working-class street. Birds chirped and chattered on the pre-dawn breeze, and a worn-out Plymouth whined slowly to a stop in front of one of these decrepit wood-framed flats. A smallish figure slipped out, ran to the big front porch, then darted back to the street.

As the Plymouth's door opened, the yellow dome light limned the black, care-lined, 38-year-old face of Joe Martino. Thirteen-year-old Lissa slid onto the front bench next to him and shut the door. In darkness again he moved the car forward.

"Your turn, Pappy." The girl reached to the backseat for a rolled-up paper in a thin rubber band.

"Pappy?" Martino's glance raised an eyebrow and made a face. "Where'd you get that? Pappy."

She shrugged, then smiled.

He said, "Okay, how about something that rhymes with table."

Her guess was quick: "A place to keep horses."

"No, it's not a stable."

Martino brought the car to a stop again, and Lissa opened the door. "How about the name of Mama's funky old aunt?"

He grinned. "No, it's not Aunt Mable."

Out of the car once more, the girl slammed the door, just the way he'd told her not to. He watched as she sprinted toward another porch. In the dome light her thin face and dancing eyes had so mimed her mother that he suddenly found it hard to swallow.

Tossing the paper up on the porch, Lissa ran back to the Plymouth, and Martino again sent it forward. This time she grabbed two papers from behind. "Is it the kind of fur coat that Mama always wanted?"

"No, it's not a sable. But that's pretty good for a kid." When he stopped the car, Lissa opened the door and eyed her father. He reminded her: "Don't slam it."

"Right. For a kid? How about the kind of story that Aesop wrote?"

He laughed. "Yeah, it's a fable."

"Oh, Pappy, that was a good one!" In the darkness she moved quickly away, carrying the two papers. Her lean teen hips in the jeans he bought the other day were hinting at the future.

At the front steps of the first house, Lissa flipped one paper onto the rubber mat and ran quickly past the next two houses, glancing at the old Plymouth whining again slowly up the street and staying just behind her. They both knew every stop without thinking.

One more to run past. But as she moved through the overgrown yard in front of a low, crumbling porch, a loud, percussive crack seemed to explode right next to her ear. Terror bolted through her body. A sharp sting seared her right arm, and the rolled up paper fell from her hand. In a panic, she froze, then spun, unable to find the street.

Another explosive crack and with a high-pitched scream she ran, finally glimpsing the Plymouth. Veering toward the street where the old car's door was swinging open, she screamed, "Daddy!" Another crack and, almost to the Plymouth, her legs stopped working properly. She saw her father screaming at her but couldn't hear him, the cracks now coming quickly one after another. Stumbling badly she threw herself at the car and somehow got her head to the seat and her left hand far enough in for her father to grab.

As Martino shoved the accelerator to the floor, there were more cracks and a side window exploded. The car lunged and squealed away, and, covered with shards and fragments and feeling his right arm go numb, he lost his grip on Lissa's hand.

The car careened weirdly across the street, jumped the curb and crashed into a front porch. The impact echoed for a moment, then faded into the whispers of the dying trees.

Back on the cracked pavement in the middle of the street Lissa was sprawled face down.

###

For more information on this and other works by T.V. LoCicero

please visit:

www.tvlocicero.com

www.ingramcontent.com/pod-product-compliance
Lightning Source LLC
Chambersburg PA
CBHW020613180626
46810CB00007B/2750